Face of Glass

Damon L. Wakes

To Ali,

Hope you enjoy!

Damon L. Wakes

ACKNOWLEDGEMENTS

It would be impossible to acknowledge all the people who have supported this book. However, thanks must go to G. Deyke, Barbara Berrington and Robin Gray for their invaluable feedback, to Laura Knowles for the cover, and to my mother and father, for a great many things. Also, the Office of Letters and Light, who provided a great deal of support for the first draft, and the Pitt Rivers Museum, whose fascinating collection of head trophies gave me the inspiration for so much of this book.

CONTENTS

1   The Boar   1

2   The Messenger   5

3   The Merchant   12

4   The Power of Steel   20

5   The Chieftain's Gift   29

6   Mountain   34

7   Knucklebones and Gourds   38

8   The Warlock's Price   46

9   Bones and Strings   51

10   The In-between   56

11   A Spirit Speaks   62

12   Second Thoughts   68

13   The Chief Who Sold the Tribe   72

14   Fires in the Valley   77

15   A Voice Amongst the Flies   86

16   Sun   89

17   The Storm of Arrows   96

18	A Faceless Friend	103
19	Voice of Pearl	109
20	Moon	117
21	Three Tales	126
22	An Omen	133
23	The Power of Stone	139
24	The Warlock's Cave	148
25	SutaKe Returns	153
26	The Great Work	161
27	The Mask Restored	165
28	The Tribes United	170
29	The Name of the Gods	174
30	Eyes Like Flame	180

1
THE BOAR

The boar was like a thing of legend. Its nose and tusks churned the earth like water. Its hooves sank into the ground like stakes. Its breath rushed like a stream in rain. Even at a respectful distance, concealed in the scrub, ParuMe found it terrifying to watch. He tried not to rattle the bundle of arrows as he trembled: the hunters would be rightly angry if he made their presence known. SutaKe, as honour demanded, drew his bow first.

How the chieftain could see through his mask to shoot, ParuMe didn't know. Formed from a single, flawless piece of stone, the mask was a marvel that no craftsman could copy. It had been a gift—the Storyteller said—intended for the moon itself, and he could well believe it. The mask was the perfect likeness of a human face, carved and polished into sacred stone, and in many ways it was better: that black mask would never show any spasm of pain or look of fear. But for all its beauty, for all its impossible flawlessness, it looked like a suffocating and heavy thing to wear. However, when SutaKe drew his bow, he did so with the ease of any warrior, and directed his arrow as though the mask's eyes were his own.

The arrow, tipped with obsidian and guided by the best red feathers, buried itself deep in the flank of the boar. The animal kicked and raged, but with no assailant to be seen it could do nothing in retaliation. Turning, it made to flee the clearing, and ParuMe's heart leapt as he realised that the direction it had chosen was their own. Beside him, SutaKe moved to take shelter behind the nearest palm trunk, but KanaKa inched forwards, his bow drawn and level. As the boar continued its mad rush, he loosed his arrow low, driving it in deep beneath the heavy head.

That wound was dire, and would have killed any lesser creature outright. But the boar was great and, instead of falling, charged the bushes where KanaKa had shown himself. As it tore through, ParuMe saw the warrior lifted and thrown by the animal's vast head, his legs appearing upwards for just a moment like crooked trees sprouting among the ferns. He landed on his side, just beyond the edge of the undergrowth. Further on, the boar stopped and turned, the arrow in its chest broken by the charge.

"My spear, boy!" KanaKa stretched out a hand. "Give me my spear!"

But the boar had already begun to move. The ground shook as it hurtled towards the fallen hunter. KanaKa's spear already in his hands, ParuMe lunged forwards, driving the wide point between the ribs of the boar. It was as though he had grabbed hold of the tusks themselves. Furious, the creature turned, and ParuMe had to struggle to keep hold of the spear as the boar bucked and writhed. The force of the struggle pulled him from his feet and dragged him across the ground, but still he held tight: the long shaft of the spear was the only thing separating him from the thrashing tusks and hooves of the boar. This brief, panicked struggle was followed by a sudden stop. The boar fled into the undergrowth, the upper third of the weapon still embedded in its flesh.

"Idiot!" KanaKa stood and slapped ParuMe across the face. "I could have stopped it: and without breaking my finest spear! Now we must find where the boar went to die, and my weapon must be mended."

ParuMe let KanaKa drag the spear shaft from his shaking hands, then watched as he set off along the boar's deep trail. "Dolt," he muttered as the hunter walked away. Almost immediately, he remembered that the chieftain was standing close behind him. He turned to look, then realised too late that his guilty expression would betray him even if the offence had gone unnoticed.

SutaKe's expression, however, was as neutral as ever. ParuMe tried to guess what his face would look like beneath the mask. Probably angry but, if he was lucky, perhaps only disappointed. "Your master is a respected member of our tribe and a close friend of mine," he said. "His honour must be maintained."

"Sorry." ParuMe looked at the ground.

"...even when he does act like a dolt." Behind the mask, SutaKe might have been smiling. "Your loyalty is impressive, even if your behaviour is not. Had you let the boar trample him, you would be a free man now."

"I...I really didn't think of that."

"I imagine KanaKa didn't either. I may remind him of it later."

Together, they joined KanaKa and the boar's trail until it came to the river. Here, the boar had leapt or waded, but there was a narrower crossing place downstream. ParuMe and the hunters made this longer, safer journey, knowing that the boar could not have gone much farther. ParuMe was already halfway across when KanaKa spoke.

"SutaKe," he said. "There is a footprint here. A footprint with no toes."

ParuMe made his way back to that bank. There, sharp and clear in the dense mud, was the footprint. As KanaKa had said, it had no toes, but there was space for them. The end of the print was smooth and round. Also, the impression was more or less flat, with no distinct mark from ball or heel.

SutaKe studied it, but not closely.

"Have you ever seen anything like this?" asked KanaKa.

"I have, once before. This was made by a shoe."

ParuMe felt a shudder run down his spine. That, and the adventure with the boar, made him bold enough to speak to the chieftain directly. "Like the KasseKo wear on the mountain?" He had never met that tribe, but he had heard many, many stories.

"Like that," said SutaKe, "but no. This visitor has come from much farther away. Much, much farther." Reaching into a pouch on his belt, he took out an object wrapped tightly in hide. When he unwrapped it, it gleamed with the light of the sun.

It was a knife, but not a knife like ParuMe had ever seen. The edge was one smooth curve, like no knapped stone, and its surface shone like water. It looked as though it should have fallen from the sky—a cutting wind frozen solid—but there was also something unmistakably human about it. The wooden handle bore the marks of tools, and being undecorated seemed almost crude. SutaKe held it above the shoeprint, as though comparing the two. In their roundness and smoothness, there did seem to be some connection between them.

"Steelmen have come," SutaKe said at last.

"What do they want?" asked KanaKa.

SutaKe re-wrapped the knife and returned it to his belt. "Before long, I am sure they will tell us."

More even than when he had insulted KanaKa, ParuMe wished that he could see the chieftain's real face, and this time he felt he almost could. SutaKe's voice, flat and hard, suggested that it would look much the same as his face of glass.

2

THE MESSENGER

The boar was as formidable dead as it had been alive. ParuMe had been sent back to the village to fetch some rope and two of SutaKe's slaves, but still he had to drag the carcass with the others. Even among the five of them, and even having lashed the boar to two sturdy branches, it was difficult work. ParuMe was glad that SutaKe, unlike the chieftain of his own tribe, was willing to work like everyone else. This, ParuMe supposed, was one of the benefits of living in such a small community: every one of the HoluKo people had to do their part. The ignominy of having a master was easy to bear when he did much the same work as you. KanaKa's honour did not excuse him from lugging the boar back through the forest, and unlike so many warriors of the DanaKo, he had earned his status. The skin over KanaKa's right collarbone was marked with six scars, white and raised, and he had not been named a warrior until he had gained the third of these. Many of ParuMe's own people were named warriors on reputation alone, without having slain even a single enemy. ParuMe wondered how many scars SutaKe wore, but as his face was hidden by the sacred mask, so were his shoulders hidden by a woven collar. ParuMe had a strong suspicion that this was done to conceal his warrior's scars, if he had any. Then again, if the legends were true, the chieftain's experience in battle could not be questioned. If the legends were true, SutaKe was immortal.

The village, small though it was, was lively. Very small children played in the dust around the fire pit, very old women wove baskets in the shade, and just about everybody else tended the tuber fields. Seeing the others bringing water and digging out weeds put the day in a fresh perspective. Even if the boar was heavy and the air was hot, ParuMe was glad to have spent the morning away from his usual work. In a little more than a year, his family's debt would be repaid and he would be "ParuRo" once again: no longer a slave. That happy day still seemed a long way away, but he tried to remind himself that the months until then would be months well-spent. Deeds, as well as status, meant honour among the HoluKo, and once free he did not intend to leave them. Someday, ParuMe hoped to become an apprentice to SanaRo. He would make little things at first—arrowheads and small blades—then move on to knives and axes. After that, though not likely enough to truly hope for, he thought there might be a chance he could become a mirror-maker. The DanaKo had many such obsidian tools and treasures, but all had been earned through trade. He cast a lingering glance over at SanaRo's hut and the sparkling black chips littering the ground by the doorway.

"Father!" HanaRa came running from the field. "Father, are you hurt?"

KanaKa looked down, and it was only then that ParuMe realised that the warrior was covered in cuts and bruises. In the village, they stood out in a way that they somehow hadn't in the forest. One raking scrape in particular looked as though it might have been left by one of the boar's tusks. KanaKa laughed. "Hurt? You should know that no boar could hurt me. A warrior who has fought the KasseKo need fear nothing else."

"And you?" HanaRa took ParuMe's hand in her own, though his encounter with the boar had left him more muddy than anything else.

With a tap of what was left of his spear, KanaKa deftly knocked ParuMe's hand away. "I've told you before." There was a stern note to his voice, but ParuMe suspected any threat was directed at him. "No daughter of mine will have anything to do with a slave."

"I do nothing more than what is proper," she said, sweetly. "And he will not always be a slave."

"And then," said KanaKa, not unkindly, "things will be different. Now, if there's nothing else, this boar must be prepared. If we don't do it soon, the flies will have eaten it before we get a chance."

"Actually," said HanaRa, "there is something else. There's a messenger in the Great Hut. You've been summoned."

"You go," KanaKa said to ParuMe. "It's probably about you. When I was last in the valley of the DanaKo, there was talk of extending your service."

ParuMe's heart lurched. KanaKa's comment about things being "different" once he was free suddenly didn't sound as promising as it had done before.

"If that's what it is, tell them that such a bargain isn't proper." KanaKa held his head high. "Tell them that they cannot barter with what I already have."

ParuMe let himself relax. As infuriating as KanaKa's fixation with honour could be, it was not always unwelcome: a less virtuous master might draw out his slaves' service almost indefinitely. "I will go," said ParuMe, "but I'm afraid they might not listen to me. They might think I was only giving the answer that suited me."

"If that's the case, they can ask anyone else here: no HoluKo warrior would accept such a deal."

Setting off for the Great Hut, ParuMe hoped that was true. Then again, KanaKa's answer was really the only thing that mattered: since he would never agree to such a bargain, ParuMe realised that he didn't have much cause for concern. Nevertheless, he still found himself peeping through the doorway of the Great Hut, rather than stepping right in.

It was fortunate that he hesitated. Sitting in a ring inside the hut were almost all the HoluKo warriors—BaraKa, NaruKa, SiloKa, NovuKa—and the chieftain SutaKe at their head, who must have been called in the moment he reached the village. It must have been done quietly, too, for ParuMe hadn't noticed it happen. Though he knew nothing about politics, he could tell that this was not just some banal trade meeting. He could also, looking at the messenger, guess the topic of discussion; the messenger wore hides on his feet.

Noticing perhaps ParuMe's shadow on the floor of the hut, SutaKe's masked head turned. "Where is KanaKa?" he asked.

"He is..." ParuMe wasn't sure how best to answer. "I will bring him." He took a few leisurely steps back, then turned and ran once he was fairly sure the warriors in the hut would not hear. Whether or not KanaKa would be dishonoured by failing to attend, ParuMe was eager to know what the Steelman would say, and the warrior was his best chance of finding out. He ran to KanaKa's hut then, having no luck, ran laps around the village. Eventually, cursing his stupidity, he went to where the boar was being prepared.

HanaRa was there, cleaning the carcass. Even elbow-deep in entrails she was beautiful. Her hair flowed in waves down her shoulders, but not once did she let it trail in her work, though it wafted freely in the breeze. She smiled, looking up. "Yes?"

TulaRa, also working on the boar, covered her mouth with an arm to giggle. She too had noticed ParuMe staring.

"Sorry." He allowed a moment for a nervous smile before getting to the matter that had seen him running all around the village just a moment before. "Is KanaKa here?"

"He went to the quarry. He wants SanaRo to mend his spear. Is something wrong?" She reached out and ParuMe flinched back involuntarily. HanaRa looked down at her blood-slicked hand. "Oops." She laughed. "Sorry."

"It wasn't anything to do with me," ParuMe explained. "Don't worry. Only, all the warriors are there. All of them except KanaKa."

HanaRa looked over towards the mountain. "You might catch him, but it would take time. If the message is important, it won't wait that long."

For the first time, ParuMe felt a little guilty about the spear. The journey to the quarry was not a short one, and KanaKa must have planned to walk very quickly if he hoped to be back by nightfall. He would not have attempted it unless the weapon was very important to him. "What should I do?"

HanaRa turned back to work on the carcass, but her brow was furrowed with thought. "Go to the meeting in his place," she said at last.

"If...would it not be better if your mother went? Or you?"

HanaRa shook her head. "They wouldn't allow a woman in such a meeting."

"Would a slave really be any better?"

"A little. It's not unusual for a slave to act as a messenger, and anything would be better than my father remaining unrepresented."

"But I've never seen a meeting like this—not even in my own tribe—and I don't know the customs here. What if I said something to dishonour him?"

"You've been here long enough. And you speak at least as well as BaraKa! Perhaps your voice would benefit our tribe."

"I can't." ParuMe shook his head. "I just...come with me!" He spoke quietly, so that TulaRa wouldn't hear.

"What?"

"Come with me. They might not allow you in the hut, but if you just stayed close enough to listen...you wouldn't have to say anything unless I was about to do something disastrous. The warriors probably wouldn't even notice. Please..."

"I don't think..."

"Please! I can't do this without you."

HanaRa's expression slowly changed. She didn't normally bear any resemblance to KanaKa, but there was something in her face then that reminded ParuMe of the moment when he had slapped him. It was familiar enough that when she stood suddenly, he jumped a little.

"We have to go now." She trotted over to the nearest patch of grass and wiped her hands. She glanced back at the small group dividing up the boar, but decided she would not be missed for a little while. "The warriors have already been waiting for some time." Still somewhat bloody, she set off towards the Great Hut.

"Thank you," ParuMe managed as he tried to keep up. "Thank you."

Even looking in through the distant doorway, it was apparent that the warriors were getting impatient.

"You go," said HanaRa. "I'll wait a little, so it doesn't look suspicious."

"Thanks," ParuMe said again. He made no attempt to hide his hurry as he drew close to the Great Hut. It was bad enough that KanaKa hadn't arrived, and that he himself was late, without also looking as though he had been dawdling.

"Is KanaKa coming?" demanded SutaKe.

"No. I'm sorry: he's already occupied...other matters have drawn him away. I am partly to blame, but as his slave I will pass on anything that is said here."

"It is not enough!" BaraKa thumped a fist against his knee. "We haven't been waiting for some eavesdropper. Begone!"

SutaKe, however, was not so hostile. "Has KanaKa given you the authority to act on his behalf?"

"No, SutaKe." ParuMe made a show of bowing his head, but was really trying to find support from HanaRa. She was nowhere to be seen. "I have no particular permission, but..." he thought back to what she had said. "I believe it would be better for KanaKa to be represented by his slave than for him not to be represented at all."

SutaKe sat motionless for a moment. His mask, as always, made him impossible to read. "You have learned a great deal in your time here, and I am impressed. Please sit."

ParuMe took a place from which he could see the doorway. Almost before he had settled himself on the floor, the meeting had begun.

3

THE MERCHANT

All eyes were on the Steelman. It was not just the shoes on the man's feet that demanded attention, but his whole costume. He was wrapped in a peculiar cloth, densely woven and stained with strange colours. There was no trace of grass or reed to be seen, though fur and hide fringed his garments. On his fingers and his ears and at his shoulder there were ornaments of gold. All eyes were on this man, but it was not he who spoke.

"Oltak of the Red Turtle greets you kindly." The speaker sat behind the Steelman, but his dress suggested that he was another tribesman. Nevertheless, his accent sounded foreign. ParuMe couldn't place it: he might have been from the far south of the island, or maybe even from different shores altogether. "He greets you, SutaKe the Immortal, and he greets your people. He hopes his visit finds you well."

"This is kind indeed." SutaKe picked up a wooden bowl from the floor. ParuMe saw that it was filled with sweet nuts. SutaKe passed the bowl to Oltak, who took a nut and passed the bowl to SiloKa. Oltak put the nut in his mouth only when the warrior beside him had also eaten from the bowl. The nuts travelled the ring of warriors, and ParuMe realised that it would soon be passed to him. He could see no reason why he should not take one when so often he and KanaKa had shared one plate. Indeed, it seemed likely that to refuse would cause offence. Still, he glanced out through the door of the Great Hut. HanaRa was sitting on the ground, far away, staring back. She nodded and mimed eating. The bowl came. ParuMe took a nut and passed it on. Nothing was said.

"You must have travelled a great distance to make this visit, Oltak of the Red Turtle." SutaKe spoke to the Steelman himself, though ParuMe was sure only the interpreter could understand him. "Have you come to trade?"

The interpreter passed the question on. Oltak whispered back an answer, loudly enough for ParuMe to note the odd, guttural quality of his speech. It was incomprehensible to him.

"Yes," replied the interpreter. "Oltak of the Red Turtle has great things to barter, many great things. He thinks you will be pleased with what he offers."

"This is good." SutaKe took a cup of cold herb tea from the floor and passed it to Oltak, as he had with the nuts. ParuMe watched. This time, the Steelman could not wait until SiloKa had tasted first, but to refuse would dishonour the chief. Without hesitation, he took a sip and passed the cup on. Not so wary, then, ParuMe thought. But as the cup approached him, ParuMe wondered what to do. Not once had he drunk from the same vessel as KanaKa. He looked to HanaRa for support.

"No," she waved. "No."

ParuMe passed the cup on without drinking. Nothing was said.

The cup was returned to SutaKe. "Now," he said, setting it on the ground once more. "Let us hear the details of your trade."

The interpreter looked to Oltak for a response. "Oltak of the Red Turtle has travelled a great distance indeed. As you may know, he comes from a vast land to the North—a truly vast land—where there is great prosperity. Bountiful fields stretch out to the horizon and beyond in all directions. The people there build their homes out of the very earth, cool in the sun and strong against rain, though there the weather is always mild. I have seen it with my own eyes: this is a marvellous place."

"Yes," said SutaKe. "Such people must have a great deal to offer in trade."

"They do." The interpreter nodded. "Yet for all their prosperity, there are things they lack. The Red Turtle was moored on your island once before, and Oltak wondered at the things that grew here. He wondered at the spices and herbs, the sweet fruits and rich nuts. He was amazed by what your people could coax from the land. He remembers you." The interpreter gestured to the chieftain's obsidian mask, drawing his fingers back to his own face and looking at Oltak. The Steelman smiled and nodded in recognition.

"Are these the things you wish to trade for? We have some stock of roots and spices, and remember well the things you brought before."

Oltak and his interpreter conferred briefly, though the words went back and forth enough times that ParuMe was sure there was some subtlety at work. The interpreter spoke: "Yes, these are the things, and no, these are not the things. Oltak has a grander trade in mind: one that he thinks will serve you better than the few metal trinkets he carried with him on his first voyage."

The hut was silent. The warriors who had been whispering to one another had stopped. The Steelmen, all knew, could be as dangerous as they were wealthy, and the warriors were suspicious of any trade that was not a straightforward exchange of goods.

"What is this you suggest?" asked SutaKe.

"Oltak of the Red Turtle is impressed by what you have achieved, but he is also surprised by what you have not. He sees plants torn up from your fields that, in his country, would be prized as perfume. He sees poor land set aside for tubers where foreign grain could feed you better. He sees you struggling to grow food that wealth, gold, could so much more easily provide. Oltak has wealthy friends in his own country, and if you serve him, grow the things that he can sell, he will make you as rich as he is. There is a world beyond this island, Immortal SutaKe, and it has much to offer you."

"You propose that we work for you? That we grow things to trade for gold, and that you will bring from your country its surfeit of grain?" SutaKe's tone was not hostile, though ParuMe could sense that the warriors around him were not eager to accept such a deal. "This has never been the way of the HoluKo."

"Oltak understands that this is not the way things have been done in the past. He appreciates what an upheaval this would be. Under this arrangement, both your nations would prosper, but Oltak realises that this may not be enough reason for you to overturn the ways of old. This is why he offers such a grand gift in return."

Oltak of the Red Turtle produced a bundle of close-woven cloth the same as his tunic. Unwrapping it, he revealed a marvellous treasure. It was like the knife of SutaKe, only greater. It was, ParuMe saw, a sword—but not a sword like those of the tribes. Where he had seen sturdy lengths of wood, edged with many cunning blades of stone, this was one piece of flawless steel: the same timeless tool, but translated into something solid, practical, efficient. That blade could not splinter, would not crack, would not need care from SanaRo and his pot of pitch.

"Serve my master," said the interpreter, "and he will lend you the power of steel. Your warriors will have arms and armour the like of which this land has never seen. Serve him, and you need never again fear the beasts of the forest, your neighbours in the valley, or even the raiding KasseKo."

All eyes were on the sword, ParuMe's included. Never before had he seen such an item. It was so perfect, so complete. Even the hilt, wrapped in dark leather, seemed an inseparable part of the whole. For a long time, everyone stared and nobody spoke.

"This is but the smallest token," explained the interpreter, his eyes gleaming with sights of things beyond the sea. "There will be more—so much more—if you will only turn your efforts to serve Oltak's ships."

"This is generous indeed." Even with the mask, it was obvious that SutaKe had been moved just like everybody else. "However, such a heavy deal cannot be accepted lightly. We must all take time to consider." He stood.

Oltak conferred with his interpreter once again. "Oltak agrees. He has travelled many months to bring you this offer, and will not mind a few minutes more." Gently taking up the corners of the cloth wrapping, he draped it over the sword once again. Even so, the shining of its blade remained in ParuMe's eyes. The warriors filed out the door, and he joined them, thinking eagerly of the treasures the tribe could gain. HanaRa was nowhere to be seen—or at least, she'd moved since he'd last looked out through the door of the hut. He spotted her around the side of the building, near the forest's edge, and did his best to slip away without the warriors noticing.

"Did you hear?" he asked. "Isn't it wonderful?"

She looked at him. "No," she said. "No it isn't."

For a moment, ParuMe thought she might have been joking, but her face—again with just the faintest resemblance to an angry KanaKa—suggested that she wasn't. "Why ever not? Didn't you hear what the trader was offering?"

"I did, but I also heard what he was asking. You cannot accept such a deal. When Oltak sends riches, it will be when he wants to. When he sends food, it will be as much as he cares to deliver. Working for him, we would not even be peasants. We would be slaves!"

ParuMe slipped his hand into hers. "I have found good things in being a slave."

She squeezed it, speaking sternly. "Only because you have a good master, and only because someday you will be free. My father might not always show it, and sometimes his honour might get in the way, but he cares what happens to you—to all of us. I don't think Oltak could say the same."

ParuMe suddenly considered something. "Listening through the wall...you didn't see the sword. Oltak can offer us such power!"

HanaRa's expression changed, and this time she was as far from KanaKa as could be. She was not angry at all, only disappointed, and that stung ParuMe much more painfully than KanaKa's slap. "What good is power if it only serves a tyrant?" She went back to the boar.

ParuMe wandered near the Great Hut as the warriors reassembled. They had not been gone long. For most, ParuMe thought, the decision could not have been difficult. He thought about the sword, and what HanaRa had said, still not sure what to make of the situation. Greater minds than his or hers seemed to approve of the Steelman's offer, but he could see the danger. SutaKe was the last to return to the hut, and he didn't wait at the doorway. He sat down next to Oltak once more, signalling that the meeting could now continue. The Steelman lifted the cover from the sword, as though opening up the discussion once again. The sword gleamed.

"I have reached my decision," announced SutaKe, "but such a deal cannot be made by just one man. Others must speak." He gestured for the circle to offer its answers.

SiloKa spoke: "Though honourable, the HoluKo are not many. Oltak's wealth will aid our work. Oltak's weapons will make us strong. If there is a time for change, this may be it."

The room looked to BaraKa. "I do not trust this foreign trader. He acts with honour, he is sincere, but we do not know him. However, his offer is exceedingly generous: I would be prepared to accept it."

NaruKa's turn came. "I think we should accept. This foreign land wants things we have but don't need. We want things it has but doesn't need. This is good for both our peoples, and the gift of steel is also great." He lifted his hands, showing the obvious solution.

ParuMe saw how the group was leaning. It was hard to disagree: Oltak had simply offered too much for them to refuse. He looked down at the sword again, but noticed for the first time how little craftsmanship there was. How little art. SutaKe's knife was this thing in miniature. In its perfect sheen, he saw no fingerprints, no spirit. It was as featureless as the footprint by the river. "No." He stood. "We cannot accept this offer. If we do, Oltak will be our chieftain. No—he will be more than our chieftain—he will be our master. He will say how our days are spent. He will take all that he wants and give only what he cares. This gift..." he pointed at the wretched sword. "This does nothing to mend that."

Nothing was said, but ParuMe knew he had stepped beyond the bounds of honour. He sat down, listening nervously to the whispers of the interpreter.

NovuKa thought before speaking. "It would not do to dismiss this offer." It was not an objection. Neither did it suggest approval.

"It seems we are not in agreement." SutaKe's masked head turned to look at ParuMe, causing his stomach to lurch. "KanaKa's stand-in is almost as obstinate as the real thing."

ParuMe couldn't be sure what this meant: whether he had been useful, or whether he had made a nuisance of himself. In either case, it seemed best to say nothing more.

"Many of us would welcome your trade, Oltak, but what you have suggested would have great consequences for our tribe. I could not agree to it without the support of all my warriors."

"The interpreter translated the answer, and Oltak, with no change of expression, re-wrapped the sword.

"If you would care to barter for some spice...some smaller trade, I am sure we too could ask some lesser gift of you."

Oltak whispered to his interpreter once more. "Oltak of the Red Turtle is an exceptionally wealthy man. He..." the interpreter had to pause in order to ask something of his master. "Oltak has made a joke. It does not translate well, but he says: 'I don't think you have enough spice to sate my appetite for trade.' This is the best that I can do. Please laugh politely."

Not wanting to appear rude, the group forced a laugh. BaraKa's was perhaps a little too enthusiastic.

"Thank you." The interpreter smiled, and his master whispered something in his ear. "Oltak of the Red Turtle continues to wish you well. He says you look taller, SutaKe, than when you last met: as though you are a different person. He hopes you will not forget his generous offer. He believes you may yet wish to accept."

4

THE POWER OF STEEL

ParuMe couldn't sleep that night. Staring at the ceiling of KanaKa's storeroom, he wondered if the warrior would truly be grateful for what he had done. Acting as a stand-in, it was not ParuMe who would have to deal with the aftermath of what he'd said.

"Are you awake?" HanaRa spoke quietly, so as not to wake her mother, but through the thin reed wall of the hut it was loud enough.

"Yes."

"Thinking about before?"

"Yes."

There was a pause. "And what do you think?"

"I think maybe I should have gone along with the others. If KanaKa wanted to oppose the deal, that would be one thing. I don't know if it was right to do it in his name. The other warriors might not be pleased."

"I was thinking that too. I'm sorry: perhaps I didn't help you much after all."

"No." ParuMe smiled. "I wish they'd just let you speak

on KanaKa's behalf. You know the customs. You have the ideas. I couldn't have done anything without you."

HanaRa was silent for a moment. "You did well just to make them listen," she said, consolingly. "And maybe it's for the best. My father might be angry that you opposed a good trade, but he would definitely be more angry if you accepted a bad one."

"That's true."

ParuMe sat up and watched the embers of the village fire through the doorway. "HanaRa?" he said at last.

"Yes?"

"Don't tell your father I asked you for help. At least, not if he's angry. He's often mad at me: I don't want him to be mad at...us."

"Alright." She laughed quietly. "But only because he sometimes says things would be easier without a slave. I'm secretly hoping that he'll free you out of sheer annoyance."

He must have been joking, ParuMe thought. Then he remembered the spear, and it seemed somehow possible. "Do you think he really would?"

"No!" She laughed louder. "And I don't think you should try."

A breeze made the dull embers of the fire glow a sudden yellow. A spark drifted out and away.

"ParuMe?"

"Yes?"

"Once you're free: if you want to go back home to the DanaKo, I'll go with you."

"Thank you," he said, genuinely touched. "But...I don't want to go back. I want this to be my home."

"That leaky storeroom?"

This time it was his turn to laugh. "If it has to be."

Time passed, and the sky grew darker, but still ParuMe could not sleep. He lay awake until he thought he heard KanaKa's footsteps on the path outside. He listened, and the footsteps drew closer. It had to be KanaKa: he was being careful not to wake them, but nobody else would come so close to the hut. ParuMe thought it would be best to let him sleep, not to trouble him, especially after the long journey. However, the not knowing was worse than any wrath the warrior could dish out. As the footsteps reached the door, ParuMe decided he could bear it no longer. He crept out of the storeroom. "KanaKa," he spoke quietly, "I..."

It was not KanaKa. In the moonlight, the wooden face of some hideous beast turned to stare at him, carved teeth silhouetted against the sky. Warpaint bright against his skin, the tribesman hefted a club. Ducking hurriedly out of the way, ParuMe blundered into the reeds of the storeroom wall in his rush to escape.

From the other side of the village, there was a shout. It sounded like NaruKa. "Warriors, rise!" he bellowed. The sound of a scuffle travelled clearly through the night.

The masked warrior drew his club back for another swing, but this time ParuMe could not shy away. Instead, he leapt forwards with a shout, catching the man's arm before he could bring the club down. But almost before ParuMe could close his grip, the warrior was pummelling him with his free hand. The blows came fast, and with full force. Trying to twist away, ParuMe stumbled over his assailant's foot, pulling them both to the ground. During the tumble, he seized the chance to pin the warrior's arm beneath his knee, wrenching the club from his grasp. Another punch caught him hard in the stomach, winding him, but he already had the advantage. Driving the head of the club down hard with both hands, he caught the edge of the warrior's mask. An obsidian blade glittered for a moment in the moonlight, leaving ParuMe no time to react, but as suddenly as it had appeared, it was gone: HanaRa had emerged silently from the hut and caught hold of the attacker's other arm, holding it tight against the ground. ParuMe drove the club down again, this time hearing wood crunch beneath its weight. A second blow, and the warrior lay still.

"What's happening?" asked HanaRa. "Is it the KasseKo?"

For a moment, ParuMe thought that it was, but there was no hissing chant, no rattling of bones. Also, the terrible warriors of that tribe wore no masks. He shuffled to one side, so that his shadow no longer fell over the warrior's head. He lifted the mask, and was astounded to realise that he recognised the ruined face beneath. He did not know the name, but he had seen it many times in the fields of the valley. He turned to HanaRa. "It is the DanaKo: my own tribe."

"It can't be. Our people have always been allies. It...it can't be."

"It is, HanaRa. I know this man." He stood and looked down at the body in the moonlight. "And I know the symbols in the paint."

All around, the village had become a confused mess of activity. In the centre, a man dipped a resinous branch into the dying embers and dragged its burning ends around the base of a hut. An arrow ripped from the darkness and left him sprawling in the dust, but still the branch glowed and still the hut burned.

"Take your mother and hide in the forest," ParuMe said. "It'll be safer there." He took the hide grip of the club firmly in his hand, then set off, keeping an eye all around for sneaking foes.

In the confusion of the attack, small battles had broken out all across the village. The attackers, it seemed, were not many, but they had the advantages of darkness and surprise. ParuMe ran directly to the Great Hut. In time, he knew that the tribe must rally there, and he hoped there would already be a safe group inside. However, when he came to the door there was only one man, and he was dead. ParuMe didn't stop to check who it was. Whether HoluKo friend or

DanaKo foe, he couldn't let grief distract him now.

The light from the burning hut shone into this one, casting thin lines of light through the reed walls and across the earth floor. The light shone also across the figure who leapt towards the door. In a panic, ParuMe lifted his club, but the warrior came no closer.

"ParuRo?"

ParuMe recognised the voice.

"ParuRo, is that you?" There was a touch of threatening uncertainty in it this time.

"LoruRo!"

His old acquaintance from the valley fields stepped forward. "It is 'LoruKa' now." He gestured to a single, livid-white warrior scar on his collarbone. "I'd forgotten you had been made a slave here. 'ParuMe,' then."

"Yes." ParuMe smiled, despite himself. Even under the circumstances he found it hard to be angry with such a kind, familiar face. There was a reason for the raid, he told himself. He hadn't heard what the DanaKo had to say.

"So as one of us rises, the other falls." LoruKa smiled back. "But now that I am a warrior, I can help you: you can be free."

As LoruKa stepped forward, the roof of the brightly-burning hut fell in, sending a sudden flash through the reeds. In the new light, ParuMe spotted two neat cuts next to LoruKa's white scar, already rubbed with coarse ash from the fire so they would heal as raised lines. One, he could guess, represented the body by the doorway. As the flames of the hut died down again, he found himself looking for the kill represented by the other. It was then that he saw the obsidian mask, and the broken sword of wood and stone. SutaKe the Immortal lay motionless on the floor.

LoruKa moved to the fallen chief and nudged him with a grimy foot, provoking only a feeble struggle. "Should have taken the Steelman's offer."

Now LoruKa had turned, ParuMe could see the sword in his hand. It looked exactly like the one the trader had brought, and for all ParuMe knew, this could have been the second time it had come to this hut. With a yell, he threw himself forward, swinging the club at LoruKa's head with both hands. LoruKa stepped back, surprised, and the club only clipped the end of his nose. With as much speed as he could muster, ParuMe whipped the club back, forcing LoruKa to step again. For the third swing, LoruKa was ready, and positioned his sword for a vicious stab. But ParuMe was enraged. Heedless of the warrior's blade, he swung again, catching LoruKa in the temple as he made his lunge. It was the middle of the club that had connected, not the head, and so the blow was not powerful. It was, however, enough to knock LoruKa off balance, and enough to split the skin above his skull.

"What are you doing?" LoruKa retreated a few paces, pressing his wound with his free hand. "I came to free you, and you attack me? Me, of your own people?"

"You crawl from the dark!" ParuMe shouted. "You fight warriors with no warpaint, and you attack without battle-song! And you claim scars for this? You are no warrior...you are a coward! No steel can strengthen your quivering heart."

Now it was LoruKa who fought in a rage. He dashed forwards, his swinging sword bright in the reed-gaps' light. Steadying the head of his club with his free hand, ParuMe blocked the blade. The force of the blow nearly threw him to the ground.

"Coward, am I?" LoruKa's knee found his stomach. "You are a traitor! To think we once worked the same field. To think your hands touched the tubers our people ate!"

In the struggle, the blade worked free of the wood. But before LoruKa could use it, ParuMe swung the club at the back of his knee. He had no time to deliver a hard blow, but it was enough to buckle the warrior's leg and send him to the ground. ParuMe readied the club for a deadly swing, but had to jump back as LoruKa's sword came in low. Scrambling to his feet, LoruKa made a frenzied rush, feinting before making his attack so that ParuMe's clumsy parry would fail. By pure chance, however, the club still stopped the blade. The sword's swing had caught the head of the club, splitting it almost down to ParuMe's knuckles. He snatched his hand away, and LoruKa wrenched his blade free of the ruined weapon, throwing its remains far to one side. When next the sword came, ParuMe could only step beyond its reach. Taking advantage of this, LoruKa pushed him back farther and farther, until at last he lost his footing.

ParuMe landed on something that pressed a shallow cut into the flesh of his back. As LoruKa leapt to deliver the final blow, he realised that this sharp thing was SutaKe's broken sword, its eon-forged edge sundered by modern steel. Nicking his fingers on the sword's stone blades, he fumbled for its hilt, and as LoruKa's blade descended, he found it. Swinging up, he knew he could not block that blow. Instead, he chopped at LoruKa's unprotected arm.

The warrior screamed and dropped his sword, fingers dangling limply from his palm. ParuMe tried to gain his footing once again, but LoruKa kicked him with a force born of pain. Flat on his back once again, ParuMe struck out with SutaKe's weapon, but found LoruKa's good hand on his wrist and his foot on his throat. The angles of his contorted face jumping in the eerie light, LoruKa stepped down hard. With his free hand, ParuMe formed a fist and beat at the warrior as best he could, but his position was hopeless. The next hut over was burning brighter than ever, but still the room grew dim.

There was a thud. LoruKa's grip grew suddenly tighter, but his foot slipped. Under some unseen but powerful force, he was pushed to one side and ParuMe was free. ParuMe took a first, choking breath. KanaKa stood over LoruKa's body. With one sharp tug, he retrieved a simple wooden spear from its back.

"You..." ParuMe gave himself a moment to breathe. "You will have a new scar tomorrow."

KanaKa looked down at LoruKa with contempt. "I would not give this wretch the honour." Walking swiftly over to the chieftain's body, he shook him gently. "SutaKe? Are you there? Can you speak?"

A noise came from behind the mask, but ParuMe could not make out words.

"Fetch SanaRo—he came back with me. There is something he must do."

ParuMe hurried to bring the Stoneman. Fortunately, SanaRo was already nearing the Great Hut. Looking around, ParuMe could see none of the DanaKo attackers, though the noises from the forest suggested that some of the fighting had merely moved. He hoped HanaRa had had the sense to come back already. He trusted she had. Once SanaRo had been given his message, ParuMe made his way back to KanaKa's hut.

"ParuMe!" HanaRa was already there. Dropping KanaKa's bow—ParuMe was glad she had thought of taking it with her—she threw her arms around him, then let go, looking around sheepishly. "I was so worried. I thought...and when I knew it was your tribe...I thought..."

"I would never leave you, HanaRa. Never."

"Do you promise?"

"Of course I promise. I..."

"ParuMe." KanaKa hurried towards them. Instinctively, they stepped apart, but the warrior didn't seem to notice. "SutaKe has summoned you. You must go quickly. I fear..." he stopped himself. "You must go quickly."

"I will." ParuMe set off at a run, and was surprised to find KanaKa running alongside him.

"I tell you this not as a master," he said between breaths, "but as a friend. I believe SutaKe intends to offer you a gift. You must refuse. He is not...his judgement is..." he trailed off. "You have not been with us long. You do not know our customs well. However much you want this thing that SutaKe will give you, you must refuse it. If you do not, it will be yours forever. I do not think that would be best."

Though he knew he had to make haste, ParuMe stopped by the doorway of the Great Hut. "What is this gift he will offer?"

"I am not allowed to say. Hurry now. You don't have time to waste."

As ParuMe entered the hut, SanaRo left, but he said nothing and kept his head bowed. ParuMe looked to where SutaKe lay in the centre of the room. Rushlights had been lit now, and without the glaring stripes cast by the burning hut outside, the place seemed more normal and showed more detail. ParuMe saw that SanaRo had pressed wadding to the chief's wounds, and placed in his hands...ParuMe stopped. A chill washed over him. Resting on SutaKe's chest, rising and falling with his shallow breaths, was the obsidian mask.

5

THE CHIEFTAIN'S GIFT

ParuMe didn't know what he had been expecting, but it wasn't this. SutaKe was ancient, the Storyteller had said, but ParuMe saw only an old man—an ordinary old man—and he looked anything but immortal. ParuMe had never truly believed the legends, but neither had he expected someone so frail. The chieftain spoke.

"ParuMe?"

"I'm here." He moved closer.

"When the Steelman came, you were the only one to oppose his offer."

"That wasn't..." he almost mentioned HanaRa, then realised that to do so might cause trouble for her: had he accepted Oltak's deal, this might never have happened. For good or ill, he would take responsibility. "Yes."

"In the forest, you wielded KanaKa's spear when he had fallen."

"Yes."

"And tonight, you took up my sword when I could not."

"Yes."

SutaKe held out his mask with wavering hands. "Do so once more."

ParuMe wouldn't take it. "I don't understand."

"Warriors die. Men die. Slaves die. But SutaKe must always live. The moon demands it, and the people require it."

In that moment, ParuMe knew what he had before only suspected.

"For a tribe to lose its chieftain, that is a terrible thing. But who would miss a slave?"

Suddenly, KanaKa's warning made sudden, cruel sense. SutaKe was offering a chance to lead the tribe, but he was also offering something that ParuMe wanted far more: freedom. Now that the DanaKo had shed blood in the village, now that the peace between their tribes was surely at an end, who could say whether or not KanaKa would ever let him go? Only KanaKa. As ParuMe, he and HanaRa might never be united. But as SutaKe, who could prevent it? He remembered the expression of disgust on the warrior's face as he tugged his spear from LoruKa's back. Surely KanaKa's honour could not allow his daughter to be united with one of the DanaKo now.

"I have led the HoluKo for a long time," said SutaKe, "but the times ahead will be hard and things must change. You have learned our ways well: I trust that you will lead well too."

ParuMe hesitated, but only for a moment. His hopes for HanaRa overwhelmed his doubts about himself, and so he took the mask. "I will."

ParuMe placed the mask over his face, and stood as SutaKe. SanaRo came from his place by the door and tied its straps, fastening the ceremonial collar about his shoulders as well. In mere moments, the change was complete. Leaving the aged slave in the hut, SutaKe walked out to where KanaKa was waiting, and spoke to him.

"Have you...anything to say?" Even speaking quietly,

unsure how the warrior would react, he was surprised how his voice filled the obsidian mask.

"What can I say?" The warrior spoke politely, but the disappointment in his face was clear. "Our tribe has lost a good man today, SutaKe." That name—though it was his now—sounded odd. "Perhaps it has lost two."

SutaKe had expected KanaKa to be unhappy—angry even—but in his voice there was only regret. It was unnerving, and robbed SutaKe of any joy he might have felt at that moment.

SanaRo drew close. "This has been a difficult day. I suggest you take what rest you can: there will doubtless be further trials in the morning. Let me show you to your hut." He spoke almost as he would have done to the real SutaKe, but there was something not quite right. This charade, intended to preserve the illusion of an immortal chief, only seemed to draw attention to the new body beneath the mask.

But that mask's new wearer had chosen it for a reason. "No. It wouldn't do to neglect my people after such an ordeal." Without waiting for permission—for now he needed none—he made his way to KanaKa's hut, where HanaRa was waiting.

"ParuMe?" She was already at the door. Seeing him, the mask, the woven collar, she stopped.

SutaKe found himself unsure what to say. For what seemed like an age, he struggled to think of something that, without destroying the charade, would convey all he had thought about before taking the mask. But he could not manage to do one without the other.

A tear shone brightly on HanaRa's face. It was quickly followed by another.

"Why are you crying?" he asked.

"Oh..." she looked down at the ground for a moment. SutaKe hadn't realised how difficult it would be to maintain this illusion, even if—and perhaps because—the tribe already knew the truth. "I am crying because..." she said at last. "Because someone made me a promise tonight, and I fear he has already broken it."

SutaKe stretched out a hand. "I'm sure that isn't..."

"You're right." She took a step back, and the words came faster this time. "It isn't anything a chieftain should concern himself with. Because for you to fret over a commoner's problems, that...that would be no better than me fretting over a slave." She turned away.

It was only then that SutaKe realised what a grave mistake he had made. At the doorway of the Great Hut, KanaKa had not been trying to make him waste this sudden gift: he had been encouraging him not to throw away what he had already earned. SutaKe stumbled away from the hut, suddenly aware of all that had gone wrong. What the old chief had thought was a chance at freedom, he now saw had placed him in far stronger fetters. What the old chief had seen as strength in the meeting with the Steelman, he should have explained was merely weakness, shored up by cunning borrowed from HanaRa. Not only had he lost that which he had hoped to gain, SutaKe was not even a competent chieftain. His being given the mask...KanaKa had been right all along: it should never have been done.

SanaRo came and led him away. "Long ago, SutaKe, you told me that there are things that no one can change. Mistakes that can never be unmade. But you of all people should know that many hopeless battles are still won. I hope to remind you that simply knowing which is which can turn one into the other.

SutaKe did his best to keep his composure, to maintain the charade. "You are wise, SanaRo. What do you think of this mistake?"

He stopped at SutaKe's hut, making a sweeping gesture across the village. "I think tomorrow night we will have warriors on watch. And in the day, I will gather the tribe to hear a tale. I think it will mean more to you than most."

"Thank you," said SutaKe. "You are a good Stoneman, and a good Storyteller: few could be both, and I can be neither."

"Perhaps not, but you must be more. You must help your people, and we must do what we can to help you."

"Thank you."

There was a rushlight in the hut, illuminating the woven hangings, the sculpted urns, the ornaments of stone. SutaKe hadn't considered what riches he had won. He blew out the light. The surrounding treasures did nothing but remind him of all he had lost.

6
MOUNTAIN

*I*n ancient days when the island was new, Moon, Sun and Mountain spoke.

SanaRo stood by the morning fire, speaking loudly to the gathered tribe. He had a good voice, and nobody minded that they had heard this story before. SanaRo told it well.

In these ancient days, not long since our land rose from the lightless sea, Man talked with these three elements and was given great knowledge. But not all was good. In those days, Mountain threw out great clouds of fire, smoke and ash, so that the HoluKo became sick and their crops grew yellow. Many climbed his face and asked him to stop. Some made sacrifices in the hope that he would cease. Many tried, and all failed, until at last SutaKe came to use his cunning.

This was how the story always began, but SutaKe found it strange to hear his name: after all, this was not a thing that he had really done. Nevertheless, he could not say this, and so he listened and allowed himself to become absorbed in SanaRo's words.

Like the others, SutaKe climbed the face of Mountain. Like the others, he braved fire, ash and smoke. And like the others, SutaKe spoke. But SutaKe's speech was different. He did not plead, and he offered no tribute. Instead, he proposed a wager.

"Great Mountain!" (SanaRo's voice rang out like SutaKe's surely never had.) *"Long have the HoluKo marvelled at your size. Long have we admired your unending strength, and always are we grateful for the glass you give: the black stone from which we make mirror, blade and arrow. But your other gifts we do not like. Your fire sears our land. Your smoke chokes our lungs. Your ash smothers our tuber fields. I greet you with honour, but I intend to stop your gifts, so that fire and smoke shall no longer rise, and ash no longer fall."*

"Pitiful wretch!" (SanaRo's voice boomed even louder than before, reflecting well Mountain's might.) *"You have the impudence to come here, thinking to contend with me? I should bury you! I should grind your bones into my glass! You think you feel my wrath on your feet? You stand only on my merciful crust, which I can separate at will, and send you down to fiery doom. What madman's fancy has made you think that any strength of yours could contend with mine?"*

"O Mountain," said SutaKe. *"It is true that no mortal could match your strength. But we small men are greater than you think. Though not your equal in raw power, our strength of will far exceeds your own, and the challenge that I have devised will show this, if you will be content to try."*

"And yet more impudence!" Mountain's sides glowed red with rage. Flames leapt high as the stars from his great head, and smoke painted the sky with black. *"What foolishness! What outrageous pride! I should swamp you with my wrath. I should send a deluge that would burn your village down. I should encase your screaming brethren in my glass, that they should remember in their last moments by whose grace it was that they had lived so long. I should do this so their blackened forms would remind you of the virtues of humility, when next you dared to sully the sides of Great Mountain with your dirty feet."*

SutaKe saw that, should Mountain's rage burn any brighter, it would indeed spill over all the island, searing everything in its path.

However, he saw also that the time had come to press his cunning. "Such a feat would surely be a testament to your strength, Great One. But it would also be a lasting record of your impatience, your intransigence, your fear."

"Fear? What do you think I could fear? Sun cannot harm me with his heat, and Moon has no power over the tides of my flames. I fear not these figures, and there are none greater on this island, or anywhere else."

"I say there is fear in you, Mountain! I think there is fear in you as much as flame: not only do you refuse my challenge, you are too afraid to hear it! What greater coward could there be?"

Mountain's ire cooled a little. "You are mistaken, mortal thing. I do not fear your challenge, and so I will hear it. But first I will hear what prize you offer, and what prize you demand. Be warned, however: I will never stop up fire and smoke and ash. These are the things it is in my power to produce, and never shall I stop up all three. You must choose just one, though I do not think you can win it from me."

SutaKe realised that he could not argue with Mountain on this point. Neither did he need to. He answered immediately. "I choose ash. Our crops die beneath its choking grasp: if we do not have food soon, I fear your smoke and fire will no longer be much bother."

"Very well," rumbled Mountain. "Then I choose my prize. If I win your contest, smoke and ash and flame shall all be doubled—I will have you know that until now, my compassion has held back my power—and your body will be my tribute. I will roast you slowly, so slowly. You shall taste my flames until the end of time."

"I agree to your terms, Mountain."

"Then tell me of your challenge."

"You have the strength to pour forth fire, smoke and ash. But I do not think you have the strength of will to stop. We will each of us hold our breath: whichever of us holds out longest will be the winner, and take the other's prize."

Mountain laughed, spitting embers like inverted comets across the sky. "You are a fool, SutaKe. I am immortal. The things I do, I do because they bring me joy. Fire. Smoke. Ash. These are not things that I need: but you need air. You shall die before I yield, mortal, but do not think that death can save you. I am good friends with Moon, and your spirit shall not be allowed to travel on to the white island if I forbid it."

SutaKe shuddered to think of this. He feared death like all mortal men, but to be refused a new life on the white island of Moon...that was something more terrible still. But SutaKe was confident. "You underestimate us mortals, Mountain. My breath will last me longer than you think."

"Will it, now? Well know this, SutaKe: I do not underestimate your cunning. My breath can be seen from anywhere on the island, but my eyes are not strong. I do not think I could see yours. How can I know you do not cheat?"

"I shall dive into the lightless sea, where there is no air to breathe."

"Then do it. Your feeble challenge has already wasted too much of my time." And with that, Mountain became silent. Smoke, ash and flame all stopped, and he watched SutaKe fiercely until the man dropped beneath the waves.

Mountain watched the shifting waters a long time. As the seconds slipped by, he pitied the feeble man, sure to lose the wager he himself had set. As the seconds became minutes, Mountain became impressed. The man would not win, but his attempt was honourable. Minutes became hours, and Mountain was astonished: this mortal might almost be a worthy opponent for him. Hours became days, days weeks, weeks months and months years. It has been eons, now, and still Mountain holds his breath, still with stone eyes fixed tightly on that place where his rival plunged beneath the waves. Nothing in the waves there will ever escape Mountain's sight.

But there is much that Mountain did not see. He did not see how SutaKe swam through hidden caves, and he did not see how the HoluKo greeted him when he emerged. Never again has there been such a lavish feast, and never since has smoke risen or ash fallen. SutaKe has taken Mountain's power, and Mountain can no longer speak.

7
KNUCKLEBONES AND GOURDS

The legend SanaRo had told was still fresh in SutaKe's mind when the Steelmen came. They marched from the forest as a single creature: feet moving in unison, shields one unbroken line. Even through the mask's dim eyes, it was like looking at some great mirror. As they stepped from the trees, half a dozen steel heads blazed with the sun's reflected glare. Oltak was not with them, but his interpreter was. The soldiers stopped, separated, and stood.

The interpreter spoke. "My master has heard sad news," he said. "He has been told that some native neighbour has attacked your tribe. He will be glad, Immortal SutaKe, to hear you are not hurt: though I think he dared not hold such hope. In light of these bad times, he offers the HoluKo a gift," the interpreter held out a sword like before, "and a reminder of his offer, which he is sure will secure their safety. With Oltak's support, your warriors could be as strong as these." He gestured to the thin ranks behind him.

SutaKe felt a rage boiling within him that could rival that of Mountain himself. Taking the few steps necessary to reach his hut, he retrieved the sword that he had claimed from LoruKa. Walking back, he held it high, letting its bloodied edge shine in the sunlight. "Tell your master we have no need of his gifts, and we know well what his offer would entail. We have seen what evils both will bring."

The interpreter's eyes were wide. Behind his mask, SutaKe smiled. He saw now that, though the night's events had been tragic for his tribe, they had been disastrous for Oltak too. He had not known what good friends the DanaKo had been to the HoluKo before that night, and he had not realised that LoruKa would be thoughtless enough to bring steel to that battle. Oltak had hoped to secure this trade by deception, but now the truth was all too clear. His show of strength was now a clumsy threat, his spokesman's speech hollow and insincere. Had the man's face not shown all of this, his actions would have left no doubt. He burrowed back between the steel-clad warriors, trying first to escape the eyes of the tribe, and then the stones that rattled out from around the huts.

Though each individual was strong, Oltak's warriors were few in number. SutaKe could see that they had not expected to encounter force, and could guess that Oltak had not wanted to send too many, in case their visit looked like an attack. Facing the whole tribe, these six warriors found their metal no advantage against even unsharpened stones, and they beat a hasty retreat into the forest, back to wherever Oltak had set up his camp. A cheer went up around the village.

"Well, SutaKe," said SanaRo. "That's one victory. How do you plan to win the next?"

What little joy SutaKe had found in the confrontation evaporated instantly. Even against the DanaKo alone, there was little hope—that tribe was far, far larger than the HoluKo—but with Oltak's weapons, too, and his foreign warriors? Looking around, he could already see despondent faces: others were thinking the same as he did. SutaKe knew no plan that he could offer, no power he held, could provide defence against these new foes. But the legend of Mountain was still clear in his mind. That tale told of hope where none could be seen, but beyond that, it offered an idea. A solution. Stepping close to the fire, he addressed the tribe.

"My people! By all means, be happy that we have escaped this danger, but remember also that there are more threats to come. The DanaKo will be as great an enemy as they were a friend, and with the power of steel they will be greater still. They are greater than us in all but honour."

A murmur rumbled through the crowd. SutaKe knew that it was not usual for a chieftain to admit weakness, even when the enemy had the upper hand. But Oltak, they had seen, used tricks. The truth, he knew, could set him apart.

"Yes, that tribe is stronger than the HoluKo, but so was Mountain. We can overcome with will that which would overpower us with strength. That is why I will go to Mountain once more, this time to speak with RanaZo."

A louder murmur passed through the tribe. SutaKe could barely make out words, but he knew the objection. The warlock's cave lay deep within the hunting ground of the KasseKo. Even the strongest warriors around the brightest fires feared a visit from that tribe. To venture into their own lands was almost unthinkable. SutaKe looked out around the crowd, and caught sight of HanaRa. The worry on her face was plain, and it hurt him to think that he was the cause. But she was half the reason he would speak to RanaZo: the warlock knew a great many things, and not limited to battle or the white island of the night.

"I will go with you," said BaraKa, an offer that was repeated by all the other warriors of the tribe.

But "No," said SutaKe. "This is my risk to take, and besides that I think it would be safer if only one were to make this journey. One might go unnoticed, but no number of warriors could provide protection against the whole tribe of the KasseKo." And so, without a retinue, SutaKe began his journey.

No trails led into that cursed heart of the island, and those that drew near were overgrown, trod more by boar than human feet. SutaKe's journey was long, requiring a night spent in a tree not far from the KasseKo border, but what weighed on his heart was how little land truly lay between his tribe and these ever-present enemies. A costly war with the DanaKo had long ago discouraged them from venturing too far towards that side of the island, but he knew from traders' tales that the KasseKo were as deadly as ever. Their violence had not waned, but instead merely shifted south of the mountain.

Still, the forest here was calm, though the dense plant growth and lack of paths made the journey difficult indeed. SutaKe began to pick his way along a narrow little stream that, while he didn't know the area, he was sure must naturally flow down from the mountain. There was a marsh nestled in a curious hollow beneath its slopes, and the brimming soil there sent a number of weedy streams winding through the forest towards the coast. The gravelly bed of this one gave a solid surface to walk on, and—an even greater benefit—held no footprints. In this way, travelling against the course of the water, SutaKe passed much of the journey without incident. Then the chanting started.

The voices began as something wordless, barely distinguishable from the wind in the trees. As they grew closer, however, SutaKe could make out rhythm and some refrain, though the words were of a language that only the KasseKo still could speak. Seeing heads and shoulders swaying between the forest trunks, he dropped onto his stomach, feeling the cold water of the stream run across his skin and the earthy smell of woodland rot fill his nostrils. Rolling to one side, he took the steel sword from his belt. If he was discovered, it would offer him a chance to flee:

nothing more.

The chanting came closer. There was an echo to it now, something that made it seem as though it was a hundred hunters walking through the trees, not the four that he had seen. Their voices were soon joined by the rattling of knucklebones in gourds, eerily rhythmical and shaken in time. The sun beat down through the space where the trees thinned to meet the stream, but the noise of the KasseKo made the air seem dark and cold as night. SutaKe shivered in the water, a chilling film trapped behind his mask. The hunters' song brought only one joy: it meant they hadn't seen him.

Suddenly, something burst from the undergrowth into the stream. SutaKe in a panic began to rise, then stopped himself. Trotters and a tail vanished into the foliage of the other bank, causing a commotion among the leaves and in the voices of the hunters. The hissing chant morphed into shrieks as the KasseKo gave chase, breezing through the dense forest with impossible speed. SutaKe, still trembling in the water, watched as the butt of a spear slammed into the streambed, the hunter levering himself across in one uninterrupted motion. There was a storm of rattling amulets and pounding feet, and then the hunters were gone. SutaKe spent the rest of the journey more watchful even than before, but he saw no more of the KasseKo, and as far as he could tell they saw nothing of him. RanaZo's cave lay well beyond the reach of the trees, looking out over the forest from high upon the mountain. SutaKe found himself travelling once more on well-worn tracks. He knew that few outsiders would dare to make this journey. The KasseKo themselves, however, came here often. The winding pumice trail had been crushed flat by many hide-shod feet. As the last of the earth gave way to stone, SutaKe was forced to don shoes of his own. They were nothing more than scraps of boar-hide secured about his ankles, but on the rough ground they were an absolute necessity. The exposed trail did nothing to ease his journey: always he had an eye on the trees, watching for anyone who might be watching back.

Eventually, he reached the cave. The low entrance had been painted all around with swirls and symbols, worn by the wind but still clear enough to stand out against the undecorated rock. RanaZo and his predecessors had been living here longer than any could remember. As SutaKe stooped inside, he saw strings of withered heads—the hair of one stitching shut the mouth of its neighbour above—and realised that these must be gifts from the KasseKo. In the corners of the cave, there were piles of skulls, perhaps given before the art of preserving faces had been discovered, perhaps simply too old for the skin to have survived. Allowing his eyes to adjust to the gloom, SutaKe looked around for the warlock.

"It is not proper for a visitor to enter without speaking."

SutaKe jumped, bumping his head hard on the low ceiling, and had to reach up to check that he had not cracked his mask. He had thought for a moment that it had been one of the severed heads that spoke, but he saw now that it had a neck and a body—if not much of one.

A hand, nails long as rushlight reeds, stretched out towards a conch set on a low stone slab. "Give your greeting! Else I shall have to speak out of turn." The fingers drummed out a lively tattoo upon the conch. "This cave might not be good for light, but it carries sound quite nicely, and this shell's voice is louder than my own. I think the friends it brings would not be friends to you."

SutaKe knew there must be some word required, something that a chief should say before consulting the warlock. However, he had no idea what it was. "Forgive me," he blurted out instead. "I wasn't sure that you were here."

"I am always here," RanaZo croaked. "Like you, my calling is as old as time...though you are a younger SutaKe than I expected. Has some disaster struck the HoluKo? Has the Steelman's visit caused you harm?"

SutaKe sat before the small stone slab, opposite the warlock. "Your powers make you wise, RanaZo."

"I am wise without them." The warlock placed his hands upon the table and leaned forward. "SutaKe is only young when times are hard, and the stream you lay in has not washed all the blood from that trader's sword." He stretched a bony finger—and its curling nail—out towards the mouth of the cave. "This is the view that greets my eyes, but I have ways of hearing news from far beyond that horizon. The Steelmen have been here longer than you know."

"Then..." SutaKe was hopeful. "Then can you tell me more about this foe? Is there some weakness in his heart? Is there some flaw in the power of steel?"

"Bah. These are things my eyes cannot see, and my servants do not hear. To answer these questions, I must use my powers. But before that, I have a question for you." He sat and waited.

"Ask it," said SutaKe, when he was sure this was not merely a pause.

"Why do you fear the KasseKo?"

SutaKe had to stop and think. Not because he didn't know the answer, but because he had no idea why the warlock would ever have to ask. "Because they hoard bones. They wear the skins of their enemies. Because they do..." he gestured to a chain of withered heads dangling from the roof of the cave "...this."

"And do you know why they do..." RanaZo parodied his gesture with a taloned hand "...this?"

"Because they think there is magic in it."

"They don't just think that, child." The warlock grinned, and SutaKe saw that his teeth had been filed to points. "They know."

SutaKe looked around at the grisly trophies, seriously doubting that they possessed anything greater than the power to disgust. "Even if that's true, it doesn't make it right to do it. The HoluKo would never do such a thing."

"The only difference between you and the KasseKo is that they have the decency to know what they do. You'll come to me when you need help—you're happy to use my magic then—but you give me nothing. The KasseKo bring me food. They bring me tribute. They're a great deal better to me than the rest of you 'civilised' tribes. Have you ever considered that you are to the Steelman what the KasseKo are to you?"

SutaKe had never even thought to make the comparison. "That's not..."

"Oh, it is. Embrace it! That trader's spices and perfume do nothing more to set him above you than your stone mask does to set you above your neighbours here. But he thinks they do, and in time, that will make him fear you. With my magic, you will have taken the first step."

"Very well." SutaKe could see that he would get nowhere by arguing. "And what must I do after that?"

"That," said RanaZo, "is another question that wants my powers. But to answer it, I must have certain things. I need a potion to visit the In-between: this is not something that can be done at will. You must bring to me three powerful things: five bees drowned in honey; a toadstool that grows at the top of a ladder; and a frog that carries a dead man's head upon its back."

SutaKe knew where to find the first two of these things—the toadstool, he was sure, was of the sort that sprouted from the strangler fig—but was not so sure about the third. "Where can I find this frog?"

"Not beyond this island's borders, and nowhere you would not expect." This was the only answer he received.

"Please," he said. "No more riddles: I need this magic quickly."

RanaZo smiled, teeth glinting like a shark's. "With that riddle," he said, "the magic has begun."

8
THE WARLOCK'S PRICE

SutaKe found the toadstool on his way back to the HoluKo. The bees and honey were even easier to obtain: KanaKa had spotted a nest on a recent hunt. The frog, he did not know where to find. He did, however, know who to ask.

"SanaRo," he said, finding the Storyteller chipping stone outside his hut. "You know a great many stories: do you happen to have heard one about a frog with a dead man's head on its back?"

"No stories," replied SanaRo, "no. But I think I have seen such a frog."

"What?" SutaKe was too surprised even to be happy: with the other two ingredients so easy to come by, he had been sure that some trick lay in this one.

"You ask me as the Storyteller, but it is as the Stoneman that I see this thing. By the quarry, there is a pool—very marshy and overgrown, and almost not a pool at all—and it swarms with many little frogs. They're a very bright green, with an even brighter blotch of red upon their backs: a blotch that looks almost exactly like a little skull."

This was much as SutaKe had guessed it would be—he had hardly expected to find a frog carting a severed head around on its back—but still he was suspicious. "Is there anything special about these frogs?"

"There is indeed. That skull is not there by chance: pick up such a frog, and your palm will tingle. Taste it, and you will die. The people poisoned in this way do not die straight away: they rock and flail, as though the spirit has gone somewhere that the body cannot follow."

It was then that SutaKe understood the warlock's plan. It was the frog that mattered. Bees and honey, fungus from the strangler fig: these things might be only for show, or just maybe to dilute the power of the frog. In any case, he wondered if the warlock's magic was even necessary. It was the potion, he was sure, that let a man visit the In-between. But without knowing how to brew it, he still needed RanaZo, and more than anything he needed the skull-back frog. "Could you take me to this pool?"

"Of course."

"Tomorrow?"

"If that is when you wish to go."

"I think it will have to be. I have spent days travelling already, and we don't have time to wait."

A peculiar expression crossed SanaRo's face. "Did the warlock tell you anything that...changed anything?"

"RanaZo told me a lot of things, and some might have been important. But without giving him the things he asked for, I don't think they'll be any good to me. I think he knows more about Oltak than he was willing to tell. The toadstool and the frog, I think he needs. The honey, however, I suspect might just be the price we pay for what he knows."

"Ah, SutaKe." SanaRo smiled. "You should know that magic doesn't work like some little friendly trade. If he was just a trader, you'd give what he asked for and take what you wanted. But a warlock isn't like a trader. No, he makes you bring honey so that it will seem like a trade, but always he takes more from you in the end. His true exchange is power, and since you do not possess the power of magic, you will never be able to repay your debt."

Even with his mask, SutaKe's surprise must have been apparent.

"I don't mean that it's a trick," SanaRo explained. "RanaZo can do things that we never could alone, and he is right to ask a heavy price. Facing such a foe as we do now, I think it is one worth paying. But you must know that he will ask for more than honey, valuable as that gift is."

"So what exactly is this price?"

SanaRo shrugged. "That is for the warlock to decide. Most likely he will ask you to do things that the KasseKo could not—sending messages, bringing things from the coast—things outside their territory, or things that need the trust of other tribes. Be aware that the tasks he gives to you may be immense, but be aware also that the HoluKo will be there to help you."

SutaKe was glad then that he had put off asking the warlock about HanaRa. If that would mean another trade, he wasn't sure he could place another such burden on the tribe. "And what if I must use the warlock's powers twice?"

"Then you will be twice as deeply in his debt. We have managed to avoid such a trade for a very long time, but if you think two are necessary, then we must pay the price."

SutaKe knew that he couldn't do that. Not for himself, and not even for HanaRa. Still, he hated the idea that there might be some solution he had failed to see, and that the warlock might be able to provide. And RanaZo's price was too high to be fair. "What if I did not do everything he asked? It is a difficult journey to the mountain. Messages must often get lost along the way."

"That is never worth the risk." SanaRo's voice was harder than SutaKe had ever heard before. "There are tales of chiefs who bother RanaZo with too many questions, then refuse to pay his heavy price."

"And what do those tales tell?"

"Always the same story: that the KasseKo owe the warlock a great many debts, and that they are only too happy to punish those who will not pay. Entire tribes have fallen in this way."

"Then I will ask no more than I must." He looked out towards the coast, wondering how close the Red Turtle waited. With the DanaKo already serving the Steelmen, it was far too dangerous to send a scout. "Difficult days give me an easy choice to make: without RanaZo, I fear this tribe cannot survive."

SanaRo raised a hand to pat him on the back, then stopped, awkwardly. In this conversation, SutaKe had not played the part of chieftain well, and for a moment SanaRo had seen only KanaKa's slave beneath the mask. He let his hand drop, and spoke instead: "The warlock acts with an honour that the Steelman does not. There is no shame in asking his advice: the battle will still be ours to fight. Tomorrow we will do what we must, and after that we will do what we can." He left.

SutaKe turned to go back to his hut, but stopped. HanaRa was there.

"I made you this, for your journey," she said. She held out a plaited cord, three small corked gourds woven into the bottom. "I'm afraid I didn't have long to work."

He took the cord. It was a simple gift, but one that was most welcome: it would carry the warlock's ingredients while he travelled, leaving his hands free, and when the KasseKo could appear at any moment, that might make the difference between life and death. And...a sudden realisation touched him greatly. "I have been back less than a day. You must have started this as soon as I brought my news."

"I started it even before then. It was to be a new net for the fishermen, but this is more important. I know you wouldn't go to the land of the KasseKo, wouldn't see the warlock, if it wasn't for the good of the whole tribe."

"I would make that journey for far less, if I could. I would make it to ease the worries of just one commoner, if only the price was mine alone to pay. But it isn't, HanaRa. The things I do now, I must do for all of us, and nothing less."

"I understand. And that is why I help you: not as just one commoner, but as the tribe. Even if...even if things never change, that will always be the same."

The sadness in her face made SutaKe glad he had the mask, if only for that moment. "Things will change," he said firmly. "Maybe not soon, but somehow. I'll make them change. I promise."

"I've had promises broken before." She smiled, despite the tears.

"Not this one. Not if there is anything I can do. I'll keep trying."

"Then I'll keep waiting. Even after the Steelman is gone."

9

BONES AND STRINGS

SutaKe had not often made the journey to the quarry. The path was wide, and grooved with marks where branches had been dragged, heaving great quantities of stone. Though SanaRo was the tribe's only Stoneman, he often had help working the quarry and these many sets of feet had packed the trail down well. Through this great gap in the trees, the sun beat down hard.

The quarry itself was even brighter. A huge clear patch had been cut around the exposed outcrop of volcanic stone, which glittered with broken black shards and sparkled with smaller splintered chips. The things SanaRo made—the arrowheads and knife blades—looked as though they had been broken from the earth, and indeed they had been: here was the proof. Suddenly aware once more of the mask's glass eyes, he wondered if this was where it had been forged by the mountain. He wondered even if this might be the place where it had been shaped and polished. The quarry extended even beneath the shade of the trees, and beneath that cover he could see stacked stones: the remains of some ancient building. This quarry, he felt sure, was as old as the island itself: older than the HoluKo, and certainly older than his mask. He was so struck by the idea that he almost forgot why they had travelled there.

"The pool is this way," said SanaRo, turning towards the edge of the clearing.

SutaKe followed, the three gourds dangling from his shoulder. Two had their burden already, and with any luck he was about to fill the third. But it was not to be.

"It's dry." SanaRo stood in the middle of a bed of reeds: clearly a wet patch of ground, but not a pool by any means. "There's usually water." He sounded apologetic. "There's sometimes even a little stream..."

SutaKe considered that they had not had rain for quite some time. The pool that SanaRo had seen had simply been drunk up by the thirsty ground. He parted the reeds and poked at the gritty mud below. Crickets chirped mockingly in the grass: the land was dry. "Think carefully, SanaRo. Is there another pool here? Is there anywhere else these frogs might be?"

SanaRo put a hand to his eyes and looked out through the trees. SutaKe looked too. There was nothing he could see that would suggest wetlands. "No," said SanaRo. "No, not here. But we could follow the dry stream uphill. It flows out of a marsh near the foot of the mountain, but..."

SutaKe knew all too well about that place.

"Would the KasseKo be there now?"

"It's impossible to say. Unless they have bones to clean, probably not. But their village moves, and that place does have water."

SutaKe thought about it. The fastest route to RanaZo lay across that marsh—he had been considering taking it anyway—but the idea of wading through it searching, staying for any length of time...he shivered, and the mask couldn't hide it.

SanaRo saw it. "There are other places," he said. "We

could circle round with the coast. I know of a river near..."

"There isn't time." SutaKe remembered how soon after the attack Oltak's interpreter had arrived in the village. Wherever he was camped, it could not be far from the HoluKo, and it certainly wasn't far from the DanaKo. "If that merchant wanted to attack, he'd have done it by now: the only thing stopping him is the possibility that we'll change our minds and become his servants. We need this magic before he's done waiting, and I don't know how long we have. We must risk the marsh."

"If that's your decision." There was something in his voice.

SutaKe stopped. "You should go back. We will need new blades soon, and the tribe can't risk losing you."

"Perhaps you should not take your chances with the KasseKo either. Send someone else to find the frog. BaraKa has time and again..."

"There really isn't time." SutaKe wished there was some other way, but he was already afraid that he might return to find the village razed. "RanaZo will only speak to me, and I cannot wait for someone else to make the journey back from the marsh. It would waste days we do not have."

SanaRo could see the sense in this. "The streambed should be obvious all the way to the marsh," was all he said. "Be careful."

The dry streambed was not really a streambed at all. It had probably never even had a stream: just the sudden wash of water that came across the ground with heavy rain. But still, it had direction, and following its barely-defined banks uphill, SutaKe slowly neared the marsh.

It came upon him gradually—tufty pockets of reeds poking up from hollows in the ground—but soon it was a sucking mire stretching out as far as he could see. He knew, however, that it must end before the base of the mountain, and that was not so far away. Finding the area quite wet enough for frogs, he began his search.

SutaKe always kept one eye out for signs of other visitors to this place. That was how he saw the bones. They lay, tied by cord, in neat little lines across the ground, all in order: ribs, spines, legs, shins. At first, SutaKe had been as horrified to see them as he had been the strings of heads in the cave of RanaZo. But looking closer—driven by revulsion as much as curiosity—he spotted two big skulls. These bones were not for trophies, but for tools: they had come from lowly pigs. This was more reassuring than anything. However violent the KasseKo could be against their neighbours, at home they were much the same as any other tribe. Soon the little bones would be crushed for needles, and shoulder blades might serve as shovels. Having picked the good meat from the bones themselves, the KasseKo had set them out for vermin to clean. Here on the sucking mud, it would not take long: the insects alone could surely do it in a day. The air heaved with flies. A flash of pale green darted from an eye socket, sitting squat upon the grungy bone. SutaKe could see the blotch. It was not exactly like a skull, but it was close enough that he was sure this was the thing he had come to find.

The way SanaRo had described the frogs, SutaKe had expected to find them as a crowd. Taking a stealthy look around, however, he could see no more. Doubtless there were some nearby, but he didn't want to have to look again. Creeping forwards, hands cupped and raised, he prepared to make his catch. But the frog was quick and wary. Just as his hands began to fall—but long before he had a hope—it made a bounding leap from the skull. It followed this with further hops, flopping its way towards the trees. The creature was tiny. Under cover, it would be impossible to find. Making a wild leap of his own, SutaKe landed with his chin in the mud, barely managing to slap a hand over the frog before it raced away. Carefully securing it within his grip, he sat up, reaching for the gourds hanging from his shoulder. To his dismay, he found he had fallen on one and it had cracked. However, it was not the honey and so did not matter much. RanaZo, he was sure, would not mind if the toadstool was a little squashed. As he coaxed the frog through the narrow mouth of the gourd, SutaKe found his hands beginning to prickle and itch. He scrubbed them in the muddy water as best he could. Making his way along the more solid ground towards the mountain, SutaKe continued on his way, always keeping low, and always watching thirty steps ahead. He had been fortunate today: he would not waste it by demanding more luck than was his share.

10
THE IN-BETWEEN

A haze of thin smoke oozed out of the warlock's den, rising up to join the clouds. SutaKe coughed. The fuel on the fire smelled damp and sooty. Perhaps it had some magical significance. Just as likely it was the best RanaZo had to hand. Making one final check that he had frog, bees and toadstool all secured, SutaKe stood at the mouth of the cave.

"I have returned," he said, simply.

"I knew you were coming."

SutaKe wondered for a moment how this could be, then realised that the cave mouth gave a clear view of the entire marsh he had just skirted. There had been plenty of time to prepare. In addition to the lit fire, RanaZo had readied a number of shallow earthen vessels. Most held shredded herbs or bark, a few only dust. One in particular—of an elaborate, star-shaped design—had been furnished with miniscule shards of obsidian, fine as sand.

RanaZo followed his gaze, then snatched the star dish out of sight. "For forging zombies," he explained. "There has been little need of it since the KasseKo came."

"I've brought the things you asked for." SutaKe took the cord from his shoulder and handed the whole thing to RanaZo.

The warlock uncorked the gourds one by one. "Bees and honey: good. Toadstool from the ladder's top: good. Frog with a dead man's head..." keeping a hand ready over the opening, he tipped the gourd to let in the light, "good. These are the things you were to bring. Take this urn and set it by the fire."

SutaKe moved the vessel of water—which he was sure the warlock could never have lifted—while RanaZo fed more fuel to the flames. He also placed in the fire a number of rocks, curiously round, which soon began to share the fire's shimmering heat.

As the fire did its work, RanaZo did his. He crushed the toadstool into paste against a flat stone and scraped this into the pot. With dextrous, grimy fingernails, he reached into another gourd and retrieved the five drowned bees, dropping these in too. SutaKe noted that he did not, in fact, use any of the honey—instead setting it down well away from his squat stone table. Finally, he tipped in the little frog, clothed in its deathly skin. There were things added after that—strips of bark and bundles of herbs that SutaKe could not hope to identify—but nothing of note.

"Now," said RanaZo. "What is the answer you would have me seek?"

"I..." for a moment, SutaKe thought of HanaRa once again. He had made a promise, and this time he would not let it be broken. But he thought also of what she had said. If she could bear to put the tribe's struggle before their own, then so must he. "I must know how to drive away the Steelmen, and secure the safety of the HoluKo."

His hesitation had not gone unnoticed. The warlock ran a hand over HanaRa's cord, laid out across the table. "This is very finely woven, and so well suited to your task. Three gourds for my three things? The woman who wove it must think much of you, though no weaving woman could ever be a worthy match for SutaKe." RanaZo began to coax. "Are you sure there is no other answer that you seek?"

SutaKe dearly wanted this other answer, but the mask weighed heavy on his face. "I came here to secure the safety of my tribe. And nothing else." He said it with conviction.

"Very well." RanaZo dragged the woven cord behind his side of the table. "I will carry this one question—and only this one question—with me into the In-between."

Taking up a blackened, forked branch, he scooped a rock from the fire and dropped it into the urn. There was a great clap, like that of thunder, and a cloud of steam billowed up from the water. SutaKe leaned over to look inside, but the warlock reached across the table and pushed him back.

"Your mask won't hide you from the vapour."

RanaZo himself took only shallow breaths, and only while he was away from the urn. One by one, he dropped each stone—wobbling the air with its ferocious heat—into the pot. When the final rock fell, the water inside was already bubbling furiously. Taking a long bone wand from behind the table, RanaZo began to stir.

Combined with the steam from the urn, the foul smoke from the fire had become fragrant. Though none of its components individually had seemed aromatic, the potion's scent lent the atmosphere a richness that reminded SutaKe of fat roasting in rain. He waited while RanaZo waited. Then, when the mixture had cooled a little, he watched as the warlock dipped the wand horizontally, picking up a few precious drops. Holding his eyelid open with a knuckle, RanaZo then tilted the wand down, directing the potion's tears into his eye. This, he repeated once more. He sat back with legs crossed and pupils wide like pits. SutaKe waited as the warlock began his journey into the In-between.

RanaZo's spirit followed the steam from the urn out of

the mouth of the cave. In this form, he saw all around him. His cave behind, and the forest below, appeared to him simultaneously, one receding as the other grew large. The Red Turtle, he knew, lay out beyond the coast. Despite his age, RanaZo had good eyes, but the smoke and steam clouded his vision now, and the ethereal light of the In-between made the island ripple with colours of every hue. All things swayed and shifted in the likeness of a rainbow, swirling with the depth of polished glass: the mountain, his cave, the forest, the marsh. There was a man in the marsh now, picking at something just below the trees. RanaZo drifted down to see him.

The man was of the KasseKo, and a good hunter too. He often brought meat to the mountain, and RanaZo knew him well. The hunter had eleven fingers, and he twiddled them as he went about his work. RanaZo descended to plant his feet upon the marsh, watching as the hunter set out his boiled bones for the crawling ants and skittish little rats to pick clean. He set the bones out in neat little lines, tied by cord. RanaZo watched intently, enraptured by the shining trails of colour left by the hunter's hands. As tradition required, the ribs were set out first. Then the bones of the legs. When this was done, the hunter set the skull down and whispered a prayer. He was a good hunter, and RanaZo could see, in his ethereal state, that he glowed with a good magic too. The hunter had eleven fingers, and they moved gracefully as he prayed.

Suddenly, the fingers stopped. The hunter's head turned. He stepped away from the bones he had just set out, and looked at those already left by his tribe-brothers. Those bones had been well-scoured by the tiny beasts, and gleamed as white as any RanaZo had ever seen. But the hunter was not pleased. These bones were not laid out neatly, and did not glow with the bright magic of the In-between. Had some other member of the KasseKo been careless? Had he paid so little heed to tradition, and the fine magic that coursed through the flesh of all things?

No. The hunter stooped down and pressed two fingers to a handprint in the mud. A handprint smaller than his own. A handprint that any member of the KasseKo would have had the decency to smear away in this, the sacred place of bones and strings. The hunter looked up towards the mountain, and the little hollow where the warlock lived. There was a light there today. A little trail of smoke snaked its way out from the rock. The hunter looked towards this warm hearth fire, then down to the clumsy handprint pressed between the bones. The hunter had eleven fingers, and they blazed with the magic of the In-between.

Unslinging the bow from his back, the hunter selected an arrow. It was a good arrow, and RanaZo could see that it heaved with many strong enchantments. It was not like the other arrows in the hunter's arsenal: this arrow had a head like a dagger, and it had been carved from the femur of SobaKe. Its fletches, also, had been formed of good red feathers, well secured with pitch. Keeping this finest of arrows ready against his bowstring, the hunter made his way towards the mountain, keeping his eyes always on the flickering light of the cave entrance. The hunter had eleven fingers: he wore them on a string around his neck.

As the hunter left, RanaZo tried to follow, but he had become distracted. The mud beneath his feet was so sticky and thick that even his spirit-feet had become ensnared. He tried to lift them out, but, bizarrely, found himself growing smaller for no apparent reason. RanaZo was too wise a warlock to panic, but the mud held him fast and he continued to shrink. Still he remained calm. Stranger things had happened before on his journeys to the In-between. Besides, if worst came to worst, he would simply shrink down smaller than the fibres that held together the world and fall back into his cave. It would not be the first time.

It was only once RanaZo was just a little bigger than an ant that he saw the frog. He was still tall enough to see the pig skulls lying on the ground, and the frog hopped out of one of the eye sockets. Something about it was not quite right. It made a great leap forwards, and RanaZo saw that it was not a bright green, but a pale, boiled white. It hopped towards him, and as it did so, it grew bigger than the mountain. Finally, RanaZo began to panic. The frog opened its mouth, spewing forth a swarm of dead, sticky bees.

SutaKe woke with a start, and a lingering sense of a dream he could not remember. He had been lying on the hard stone floor of the warlock's cave, and the even harder stone of his mask had left an uncomfortable imprint on his face. He rubbed at it under the tight straps. His head hurt, and not just from sleeping oddly.

"RanaZo?"

There was no answer. The fire had died down, and the urn was almost cold, but the warlock sat in exactly the same place as before, legs crossed, long-nailed hands laid out on the table before him. SutaKe waited, but it was growing late and he didn't like to waste too much time.

"RanaZo?" He reached out to shake the warlock by the shoulder, then snatched his hand back as though burned. RanaZo was cold and rigid: he had been dead for quite some time.

11

A SPIRIT SPEAKS

SutaKe stared in horror at the warlock's body. Not for the ghastliness of the thing—the way the eyes stared and the rigid fingers arched—but for what he had lost. Oltak's ship was swaying somewhere out beyond the coast. The DanaKo were knapping blades and sharpening spears, and perhaps applying amulets to new weapons of steel. That tribe was many times stronger than his own: without the warlock's magic, he could not hope to stand against it. A greater chieftain, perhaps...but no. SutaKe had taken the stone mask for his own small, selfish reasons. The HoluKo had no great chief to lead them now.

The sun was low in the sky. SutaKe didn't want to travel through the lands of the KasseKo by night, and yet he couldn't bear to stay in the warlock's cave any longer. Still, he couldn't simply leave with nothing. His eyes fell upon HanaRa's string of gourds, the urn of tepid potion by the embers of the fire. Reaching past RanaZo, he retrieved the gourds, uncorking the one that was neither full nor broken. A sinister feeling seemed to swell from the cave floor, as though all the world was watching this theft. As an afterthought, SutaKe wrestled free the gourd of honey and left it between the hands of RanaZo: he would take nothing that the warlock would not have given. Dipping the empty gourd into the potion, SutaKe drew a sample. He knew of no other magic-men on the island—nobody who would know how to command the mysteries of the In-between—but it was the potion, he knew, that gave the power. SanaRo knew a little about such things: perhaps he would know another way. If not...SutaKe tried not to look at the dead, staring face. If there was no other way, he would try for himself.

SutaKe stepped out of the cave and began to make his way down the mountain. Under the trees, he could see that it was already dark as night, and by the time he reached the bottom of the mountain, the sun would be gone from the sky. He tried to hurry, though the ground was rough on his feet. He didn't want to have to climb in darkness. He didn't want to risk losing what little he had claimed. Lifting the gourd on its string, he examined it in the last light of the day, making sure there were no cracks, no leaks around the cork.

Suddenly, something screamed from out the sky. SutaKe found the gourd torn from his hand, shattered by this shouting bird with red feathers and white beak. The thing buried itself in his shoulder and he fell, tumbling down the side of the mountain until he reached a little plateau—mercifully close—that stopped his descent. It was an arrow, he realised, looking at the fletches that hovered above him as he lay there on his back. He could see the arrow head, too. It must have been long—long like a dagger—to extend so far up, but also SutaKe realised that the gourd full of potion had absorbed some of its power, preventing it from burrowing too deep into his flesh. His woven collar had also helped. He desperately wanted to tug it out of his arm, but knew that this would not be wise: SanaRo had told him once. He would leave it until he had returned to the HoluKo. The wound, in any case, could not be serious. He felt no pain, only a strange tingling. Inching himself over to the edge of the tiny plateau, he looked down towards the forest. He caught just one glimpse of the archer, racing between trees and rock. He was still far away, but SutaKe saw all too clearly the grisly talismans of the KasseKo rattling as he ran.

SutaKe knew he would be forgiven for fleeing this place now. The potion would have done little good without the warlock to use it. But still, this was his chance. The cave lay such a short distance above—nothing compared to the journey home—and he would have no other opportunity to claim that potion for his people. RanaZo was sure to have gourds amongst his arcane treasures, and if not, SutaKe knew that at least one of his own was still intact: the one that held honey. Surely a little extra sweetness would not rob the potion of its power? Levering himself onto his feet, he scrambled up the side of the mountain, back towards the cave. His head felt light. His feet seemed hardly to touch the rough ground. The light of the setting sun blazed with ten thousand colours, and all the depth of polished stone.

Inside the cave, the slanting light made it look as though the dangling heads had begun to glow. Vibrant wreaths of vapour seemed to ooze from sewn eyes and sealed mouths, but SutaKe had no time to be afraid. He hovered for a moment, staring at the warlock's hoard. He had to have empty gourds. He had to. But if there were gourds in that cave, SutaKe could not see them. He hovered a moment longer before the urgency of the situation made up his mind. He snatched the gourd of honey from the low stone slab, uncorking it the moment it was in his hand.

RanaZo blinked. SutaKe would not have seen it, had the warlock's eyes not become twin beacons of licking flame. SutaKe fell backwards in surprise.

"Welcome, Face-of-Glass. Welcome, tribe-chief of the

HoluKo." The words came in a cloud of smoke, thick as incense and varicoloured as a fish's scales. A buzzing of insects quietly filled the room. RanaZo sat as rigid as before, but the flames of his eyes had warmed his face, and he blinked once more.

"What are you?" SutaKe managed to ask at last. In his surprise, he had forgotten the gourd, and its contents had begun to ooze out over his hand. He barely felt it.

"A spirit." More technicolour smoke spilled from the mouth. "In life, RanaZo often used my strength. Now, in death, I borrow his."

SutaKe knew he could not stay long. Already, the KasseKo archer could be halfway up the hillside. But still, here was an opportunity that would never come again. "You helped RanaZo find answers. Can you help me?"

"I can. I can and I will. Your plight moves me, SutaKe. I have not often set my sight beyond the In-between, but I know your hardships. I see in them reflections of my own."

SutaKe ducked out of the cave and stared down the mountainside, being careful not to knock the arrow against the low stone entrance. He could see no sign of his attacker. He stepped back, leaving a chain of heads smouldering dimly as they swung. "What do you mean?"

"This island is yours by right, SutaKe. You have lived here always. You have worked its land and made it your own, and yet now a new force comes to claim it. A new force comes to rob you of your right, your power. Tribe-chief, this story is my own. With great hands did I sculpt this place. My fingerprints are in the earth and in its animals. Yet long ago, new gods came and claimed it for their own, and I was reduced to this." A blue ember tumbled down RanaZo's cheek, leaving scorch-marks in his wrinkled skin.

"What is it I must do?" SutaKe stepped forward, fingers pressed around the arrow in his flesh.

"Free me, SutaKe. Take me from this place. You think

this fight unwinnable, but I see a way that will mean you cannot lose. The DanaKo are strong, and steel has made them stronger. However, in their strength there is a weakness. They expect to march against you, if the Steelman does not call them off. They expect to win, if they march. But if you were to march against them, if you were to choose the time..." the voice hesitated, then became hurried. The buzzing of hornets grew louder. "Lead your warriors against the DanaKo! Do it now! It must be..." All of a sudden, there was silence once more. Silence, and a shadow in the mouth of the cave.

SutaKe looked at the man. He wore fingers around his neck. Bones on strings swayed about his ankles. He carried a club that was of light weight, but made up for this with a great cluster of obsidian spikes, all set in one direction. It was a fearsome weapon, not as elegant as the stone-bladed swords of the coastal tribes, but more than their rival in raw power. SutaKe reached for the hilt of his sword, but found that it had slipped from his belt when he fell. The KasseKo archer looked from the stone mask to RanaZo's dead face, no longer illuminated. There was a long, terrifying moment as SutaKe continued to fumble for his lost sword, the man continued to stare at the dead warlock, and his club continued to sway, ready, in the light of the cave entrance. The man's mouth stretched into a snarl. His eyes snapped away from RanaZo's face and back to the mask of SutaKe. With a screech, he leapt forwards, spiked club tearing through the air in a forceful swing. The weapon's spikes bit into a hanging head, sending wood shavings and teeth scattering across the cave.

SutaKe saw every particle as it traced its way through the air, trailing behind it the light of the In-between. He stepped up close against the cave wall, just out of reach of the deadly club. A skull crunched underfoot. Hand already around the point of the arrow, he pulled it from his skin while the KasseKo archer turned. SutaKe's assailant hefted his weapon over his shoulder, bending his knees and arching his back to make space under the low rock ceiling. In the moment just before the club fell, SutaKe saw his chance. Lunging forward, he drove the bone arrow up beneath the archer's chin. The arrowhead was long like a dagger, and the man fell without a sound.

SutaKe stood there while the sun finally dropped below the trees, waiting for his breath to slow. The body in front of him was perfectly still. He was, SutaKe saw, immense. His right arm was thick and strong from drawing string, the left stunted from bracing against the bow. The club, with its deadly cluster of stone spikes, would have been unwieldy in the hands of a lesser warrior. Yet SutaKe had slain him with nothing more than the point of an arrow: never meant to be used in close battle. He looked from the great war-club on the floor to the thin shaft lodged in the flesh.

"This..." said a voice, a cacophony of small wings behind it like breath. "This is how it must be with the DanaKo."

12
SECOND THOUGHTS

SutaKe returned to the tribe empty-handed, delirious and streaked with blood. His sword still lay somewhere out on the mountainside, or down in the bushes at its base. He had not remembered to look for it. He had thought, again and again, that he could hear the buzzing of the spirit's voice, but when he looked down he saw that it was only a crawling mass of flies drawn in by the honey that had spilled across his fingers. In the other hand, he clutched HanaRa's cord and its two remaining vessels, both ruined. In the dark, his head had ached with traces of the frog's venom. After sunrise, it had become twice as bad. But always behind the pain there was an echo: "This is how it must be."

It was KanaKa who saw him first, stumbling towards the village fire. There were no kind greetings: only a hurried march into the Great Hut. It was only once he was in the shade that SutaKe realised the warrior was ashamed: KanaKa saw only failure in this great success. But still, he realised that the rest of the tribe would see things this same way, and so he was content to stay out of sight. KanaKa, he knew now, wanted only to support him, and so he waited silently even after the warrior had left the hut. If KanaKa had been made chief, SutaKe thought, he would not have needed some spirit for guidance. Even behind the knowledge of his new hope, there was an awareness that all too soon he would have to lead the HoluKo in battle. "You cannot lose," that voice had said: yet still he longed for its strength to shield the tribe. He feared his own weakness now more than the spears of the DanaKo.

A figure appeared in the doorway of the Great Hut. SutaKe had expected KanaKa again, or perhaps SanaRo. Instead, it was HanaRa. She hesitated for a moment, held back by shock or fear, before coming forward with a bowl of water and a wad of soft cloth.

"What happened on the mountain?"

"One of the KasseKo came." He answered honestly. "The warlock is dead. I have lost the sword of steel..."

"Don't fret about that now." She placed a cool hand on his forehead.

"But HanaRa, I did bring back your gift." He reached around in the dust for the woven cord. "And I brought an answer. The warlock died, HanaRa, but I have an answer."

She reached under his woven collar and pressed the wet cloth to his wound. He flinched back. "How can you have an answer," she asked, "if the warlock is dead?"

"I..." There was something in the way she had spoken—as though she didn't expect him to hear—that made him fall silent. The dull, crawling pain in his shoulder made him think. What if there had been no spirit? In the morning light, half the trees and rocks had burned like the warlock's eyes. What if the spirit's plan had in fact been his own? Already he was beginning to doubt its wisdom. "Do you not believe me?"

"I believe that you have suffered an ordeal, and that we are lucky you came back alive. You have made every effort to ensure the safety of the HoluKo, and I believe that now you should think of your own health." She traced the cloth down his chest, wiping away the worst of the blood, before rinsing it again in the bowl. "But it is not my place to advise. I think you know what your warriors would say, and I think you know that what they say is best. I say nothing myself." She pursed her lips and continued her work.

SutaKe thought about what the spirit had said. Its words had told him nothing that he could not already have known. However real it had felt at the time, he could not be sure that the experience was not merely the product of an intoxicated mind. But still, it had offered advice, and even if the speaker had not spoken, the idea remained. With a clearer head, he thought it over. He had been away from the DanaKo for many months now, and so could guess nothing about their numbers. It was possible that many families had gone to other tribes. It was equally possible that they had grown: that LoruRo had been newly named a warrior seemed to suggest this. Yet still he remembered the thin arrow and the thick club. He remembered also the attack by the DanaKo. That had been intended only to sow seeds of fright, and make Oltak's offer more appealing. Only a vague notion at first, this had slowly become the most terrifying thing about that night: if all the DanaKo warriors had come for battle, the HoluKo could not have survived. The unprovoked attack in the dead of night...were the DanaKo not equally vulnerable to this?

He put it out of his mind. Against the DanaKo, the HoluKo were far too weak for any advantage to even the odds. And after their own attack, wouldn't the DanaKo warriors have set sentries out to watch? This plan was not the brave assault he had thought of at first: it was the charge of a cornered animal, more likely to drive it onto the hunter's spear than to see it run free.

"HanaRa," he said. "Leave me, please. You are right, as always. I have done enough."

She set down the bowl and cloth. "You have done more than enough. Oltak's offer is not so bad. If there is no other way, there is less shame in taking it than driving the tribe into the ground for pride alone."

After HanaRa had left the hut, SutaKe sat on the floor and thought. He wanted to do only what was best for the HoluKo. Despite his time amongst them—and despite the fact that he had been made their chief—he knew only so much about their customs, while HanaRa knew such a great deal. And beyond that, she was always so wise: SutaKe would take her word over that of any warrior. And yet, he did not want to be the chief who sold the tribe. He did not want to simply yield. Among SutaKe's many doubts, there was one that brought hope and not despair: he doubted KanaKa. There was a chance, he thought, that with this brave, bold assault against the DanaKo, he could secure his honour and defend the old chief's decision to give him the mask. SutaKe had to admit that he possessed only a little strength, but he trusted that the old chief had seen it, and he doubted that KanaKa knew it all. Oltak's offer would surely spare the HoluKo from disaster, but, just as surely, never would the tribe prosper again. In battle lay the only other hope, but it was mired in disaster. This was not a course that SutaKe alone could choose.

"Spirit?" He spoke quietly, lest anyone outside should hear. "Spirit, you asked me to free you. You asked me to bring you from the cave. If I have done that, if you are here, make yourself known."

There was no buzzing of wings. No every-colour flame.

"Spirit, please. I will bring whatever tribute. I will pay whatever price."

No sound but the wind against the reeds.

"Please. I cannot do this on my own."

Still no answer. SutaKe allowed himself to slump into a weary sleep, but even in the In-between of dreams no spirit came.

13
THE CHIEF WHO SOLD THE TRIBE

"SutaKe."

Despite his great fatigue, he woke up right away, feeling as though he had barely slept. "What..." He reached up to rub his eyes, but found the mask, as always, in the way. Had he not been so tired, he would have remembered. "What is it, KanaKa?"

"The evening meal has been prepared. I have brought you food, since you cannot eat in the open air."

The mask again. As much as SutaKe marvelled at the artefact's craftsmanship—the elegance of the outside, and the way the inner surface seemed to vanish against his skin—he wished dearly that its maker had not made it extend so low. Despite the burdens that mask had brought, despite the sacrifices it demanded, there was nothing he missed more than the small joy of sharing a meal around the fire at the end of the day.

"If you aren't hungry, I can come back later."

SutaKe thought of Oltak's offer. He thought of what he had to do. "I am not hungry," he said, "but I'll go with you.

There is something I must say, but...after the meal."

KanaKa looked him up and down. SutaKe was sure he could guess what the warrior was thinking. The journey to the mountain had been in vain. There really was no other way. He found himself hoping that KanaKa would become outraged, that he would demand screaming battle over quiet surrender. "If you think that is wise," was all he said. There was no hint of disapproval in his voice. SutaKe realised he should have expected this. HanaRa had felt the same way. She had said it herself: that he should know what the warriors would say. He followed KanaKa out to the fire, but the warrior's opinion did nothing to change the simple fact that he would be the chief who sold the tribe.

This meal was, oddly, more pleasant than the last. When SutaKe had said he wasn't hungry, he had lied. He hadn't eaten for more than a day, but the wound in his shoulder and the lingering, sweaty fever of the frog's venom meant he couldn't bear the thought of food. The company, however, was most welcome. Though he was sure his collar was stained with blood, nobody so much as stole a glance. Tubers, roast and boiled, were passed around, and a good deal of that great boar was cooked on sticks over the fire. Turtle eggs and fish, too, had been brought up from the sea, and in that brief, happy time, it was as though there were no dangers, there was no threat. It was—exactly as it should have been—as though the same chief as always had sat down with the same tribe as always, and all was well. If the warriors knew what he was planning to do, SutaKe considered, the tribe would too. Nobody judged him. Nobody even acknowledged that he would be the chief who sold the tribe.

Seeing how happily the HoluKo spoke and ate, SutaKe realised that, not only would he have to tell them tonight, but he would have to make the journey, too. Always nagging at the back of his mind was the knowledge of how long he had already waited to give his answer. How restless

Oltak and the DanaKo must have become. Having decided to make this surrender, he felt he had to do it before the next dawn. If the army marched upon their village before they had sent out the message, it would surely make their situation worse. They would not come at night, though, he hoped. Please let them not come at night. He would make the journey immediately. He no longer hesitated to risk the forest after dark: greater burdens had robbed him of that fear. The meal ended, and he stood.

"My people," he began. Almost his first proper speech, and it had to bear such news. "I have walked to the mountain and back, and to the mountain and back again. I spoke to the warlock, RanaZo. I did battle with a warrior of the KasseKo tribe." He thought of the arrow and the spiked club once more. If only this conflict could be resolved so quickly. But it was not to be. "But the warlock is dead now. There is no magic to help us. I am sorry."

Nothing was said.

"We must..."

He thought of the arrow, and he faltered.

"We must..."

The arrow had pierced his shoulder only lightly, but against his slower enemy, that same strike had been death.

"We..."

He could not speak the words he no longer believed.

"There is no magic to help us. We must fight with our own strength alone."

Once more, nothing was said, but this time the silence was due to shock, and not mere acceptance.

"The DanaKo attacked us in the night, without warpaint or battle-song. They cowered before the enemy, Oltak, and turned their unfair anger against former friends. This, they did: honour allows that we respond in kind."

KanaKa stood. "The DanaKo are many in number and strong with steel. Perhaps your recent ordeals have made the situation unclear to you." It was the closest thing to treason SutaKe had ever had to suffer. "Immortal leader, though honour allows an act such as you describe, none of us would think ill of you for seeking out some other way."

There were mutterings from the tribe. Though the charade continued—in the eyes of the tribe, SutaKe was the legend he always had been—KanaKa was a well-proven warrior and his opinion now held greater sway. But SutaKe saw his opportunity. No, there had been no spirit in the cave. That plan had been his alone, and he saw how it had to work.

"In this place, steel and numbers make the DanaKo strong. But there, in their own village, these things are weakness. They think that we are beaten. They celebrate a victory they have not earned—perhaps even this very night, thinking to march in the morning—and that is our advantage. We will strike before the steel is in their hands, and our speed shall panic their great numbers. A swift arrow is far more deadly than a heavy club."

The tribe was divided. KanaKa had spoken great sense, and many still shared his opinion. But just as many saw in SutaKe's plan the same small spark of hope that he had seen. Better, surely, to fight for that chance than surrender for none. Better, surely, not to make deals with the trader who had already tried to trick them. SutaKe looked around the crowd, the sick feeling in his stomach fading. The worried faces that stared back did nothing in his view to dim the eyes that shared his hope. BaraKa was amongst them. NaruKa too. He searched for the faces of the other warriors.

"This is clearly not a matter to be decided rashly." As always, NovuKa's mind would not be hurried. "Perhaps a meeting is in order. Some opportunity for the warriors, at least, to speak their mind."

SutaKe was about to speak, but SiloKa was too fast for him.

"If this is to be done, let it be done tonight! No talk! No

delays! Those who would do this thing must speak now, and I must be the first."

"I will!" BaraKa bellowed.

"And I." There was NaruKa, too.

NovuKa looked around. "We know that KanaKa does not approve, but I am swayed. As we need haste more now than care, I say that this is enough. If there is support enough for this to work, it is not necessary that all of us agree."

"It isn't necessary," KanaKa spoke again, "but still it is so. I spoke against the plan because I thought it was not the will of the tribe. Now I see that it is. I myself do not oppose this battle: a warrior who has fought the KasseKo need fear nothing else."

"Then it has been decided. We shall leave at sunset, and reach the DanaKo in the dead of night." SutaKe could barely remember his journey from the mountain. The wound in his shoulder hardly bothered him at all. Whatever happened now, he had made his decision, and he had the support of his people. Without spirits or incantations, he had learned to lead, and in the light of this all his fears—for that moment—washed away. But there was something still better to him than this. For even if this plan failed, even if this battle was lost, never would he be the chief who sold the tribe. In his relief, he was suddenly hungry. Leaving the chatter of the tribe by the fire, he returned to the Great Hut, and the meal that KanaKa had been kind enough to bring.

14
FIRES IN THE VALLEY

Never before had SutaKe travelled to a battle. He had seen them, of course, and he had fought that night when the DanaKo came, but this was different. Where the battles he had seen had been colourful and loud, the night was dull, and the warriors now walked in silence. And where the DanaKo attack had been completely unexpected, this journey gave him time to think about what lay ahead. But there was no way for him to guess what he would find at that journey's end. The DanaKo had no reason to fear his tribe, and he hoped that this would make them unprepared. The valley of the DanaKo, also, was a poor place to defend.

But although the valley offered little shelter, it was rich and fertile, and allowed the DanaKo to support many more people than almost any other tribe: the KasseKo were their only rival in this respect, and even then only because none could say exactly what their numbers were in the shadow of the mountain. He thought of what he had said in his speech, and wondered if it would prove true. The strength of the DanaKo would indeed have made them complacent; he was sure of that. But would that be enough to prove their undoing? In a tribe that size, even the slightest caution could provide security: they had warriors enough to spare for sentries, if they chose to post them.

The HoluKo reached the great shoulder of the valley. They stooped now to avoid being seen against the sky, though the trees and bushes should have been shelter enough. SutaKe stared down at his old village. It had never struck him before how large it was, and how far the fields had been cleared of trees. It was a proud village, and it was his home. Many times during the journey had he imagined this sight, and many times he had forced it from his mind. Here at the edge of the valley, however, he had to stop. The huts laid out below held many memories, and the thought of claiming them with bow and spear was almost more than he could bear. His family, he knew, slept somewhere below, and though no common people were permitted to defend the village, the HoluKo were full of rage and there was no knowing where the violence might spread. Also, he had no idea how many of his old kin might have been made warriors since he had been sold to KanaKa. He felt LoruKa's eyes upon him, watching from the white island far above.

But SutaKe felt also the eyes of his warriors, and he remembered the spirit's words. Here was a chance to take back this land. Here was a chance to break the Steelman's grasp. And so he turned his thoughts to more practical matters. Lights brighter than embers glimmered like pearls in the ocean of huts down in the valley, proving beyond a doubt that there were still tribesmen up and about, to feed the fires if nothing else. The flat, open fields would offer little protection from their wakeful eyes, and still less from any archers who might be sleeping—sleeping but ready— inside the huts.

"NaruKa." He turned to the warrior, whispering in case

his voice carried in the still night. "The tuber plants in those fields will be tall and leafy. The DanaKo will not spot just one person amongst them. There are people down there still awake: tell me if any are watching outside the village, or if all are merely tending to the fires."

"I will go." NaruKa did not go right away, however. Before he began his descent, he took a wide, waxy leaf and folded it over the stone head of his spear. This cover he tied fast with a fibrous stem.

Seeing him work, SutaKe realised that he would have to hide his head as he approached. The obsidian could shine like water, even in mere moonlight, and just one gleam could easily give the whole tribe away. It was a grave danger, but one often overlooked. NaruKa was a wise warrior to avoid it. SutaKe realised once again how little he knew, and how many others, better, there would have been to take the mask. He put that thought from his mind: he had led the tribe this long and this far. Whatever happened now, he had done all that anyone could do.

NaruKa slipped down the steep valley. SutaKe watched him at first, but soon even he could not see to mark his progress. Down on the low, flat land, the DanaKo would have little hope of spotting him. But for the entire tribe, it would not be so easy to remain unseen. SutaKe listened behind him as archers began stringing bows, the straining wood impossibly loud in the silent dimness beneath the trees. The sound would not carry to the bottom of the valley, he was sure, but still it was unnerving. Closer to the village, just one warrior's footstep could make all the tribe known. A hunter lined up his arrow with the light of the moon, then brought it to his teeth to straighten the shaft. The sound seemed loud enough to reach the stars. Inside SutaKe's mask, even his breathing rushed with noise, threatening to wake the DanaKo.

But NaruKa climbed back and still the village slept. No brands were lifted from the fires. No shouts went up around the huts.

"There are sentries," said the warrior. "From behind the Great Hut to the place where they keep their wood, I counted eight." He held up his fingers, each one representing a man standing somewhere below.

SutaKe did not need to look to know where NaruKa had been. He had walked those dusty paths often enough before the debt of his family had sent him to work for KanaKa. It was a central place—the sort of significant place that one would expect to be guarded—but it was not a big place, and eight guards was a lot. "I fear their chieftain has anticipated a plan like ours," was all he could manage.

"Perhaps their chieftain has." NaruKa grinned, his teeth bright in the darkness. "His warriors, however, have not. All are talking, and most have their eyes towards the fire."

"Fools!" BaraKa's reed mask quivered with rage.

SutaKe shared his scorn. A sentry whose eyes had been dazzled by flame was worse than one who fell asleep. At least the sleeper could still see a foe if he awoke, and at least fatigue could be his excuse. A guard who watched the flame simply did not care for his duty. "This is how little they think of us?" He spoke, rather than whispered, so all the HoluKo would hear. "Their sentries doubt that we would even make this attempt? We will show them their mistake."

Keeping low, the group made their way down the valley side and into the tuber fields. SutaKe was less concerned about noise now, though still he kept his head below the level of the leaves. Any one sentry could happen to hear something, happen to look out across the field. But if the ones NaruKa had seen were as careless as he said, it was unlikely that any others—even those who might keep an eye on the horizon—would be all that alert. The voices of the guards were hushed, but carried clearly through the night. Now and then there would be a laugh, hardly stifled. Shadows held their hands up to the fire for warmth. The chieftain must be able to hear them, SutaKe thought. And hearing them, he did not stop them. The DanaKo would be ashamed tomorrow: they had thought to protect themselves, but hadn't made the effort. SutaKe raised a hand to give the signal.

It was the archers who stood first, those with swords and spears instead crouching ready, low to the ground. The arrows' targets were well chosen, and those guards in view dropped without a sound. But one was spared—one who had been hidden by the smoke and light of a little fire beside a hut—and he ran forward with a shout, charging for the nearest archer to have lifted himself from out the sea of crops. The sentry's brave assault more than made up for his lack of vigilance, but did nothing to drive back the HoluKo. His path crossed KanaKa, still hidden amongst the tuber plants, and the warrior needed do no more than to lift his spear—newly mended by SanaRo's hand—to end the honourable charge.

Wordlessly the HoluKo hurried through the crops, circling the village. The alarm had been raised, the attack was known, but without seeing their assailants the alerted guards could do little to repel it. Two figures dashed out from amongst the huts, war-clubs hefted ready. But by the time they reached their fallen comrade, no enemy could be seen.

"Bring a light!" Even the hushed voice rang out clearly through the still air. "From the fire! Quickly!"

One of the figures darted away between the huts, then back to the other with a burning branch. In its light, the waiting archers saw them both.

This, SutaKe found, was the great weakness of the DanaKo. Few other tribes could afford to keep fires burning through the night. Most were content that theirs should die and be re-lit each day. But the DanaKo could go a great distance for wood and could afford to trade for good, long-lasting fuel. Had their warriors faced a more direct assault, and had their attackers ventured right into the village, those lights would have aided their defence. But in this battle they favoured the archers who remained unseen. Many more guards took up brands before the danger was recognised, sometimes even from the hands of bodies groaning on the floor. By the time they had finally thought to douse those fires with sand, a dozen more had been started in the tuber fields, set by the torches of fallen guards.

The great size of the village here proved to work against them once again. Determined to defend the huts, the remaining warriors of the DanaKo spread out around the fringe. Though darkness helped protect them from the archers spaced about the crops, they often strayed too far towards the fields and blundered into SutaKe's troops. The village was awake now, but not outside: well did SutaKe remember how he had been told, on such an occasion as this, to remain inside the hut. The unarmed villagers would all defend their own strong ground, but were they all to mill about, there would be chaos. But the DanaKo had been caught unawares, and so chaos reigned already. If the whole village came to fight, if all beat through the crops with lengths of wood, they could have driven back the assault. Instead, one by one, the warriors fell, until the few that remained gave up the village border and dropped back to form one mass around the great fire pit, yellow flames still lifting from the embers in the breeze. Steel spearheads glistened in the light, and steel helmets caught reflections, but they were pale now. In the moonlight, knapped stone had lost none of its sheen.

"Throw down your weapons!" SutaKe hoped that the battle would go on no longer. There was no telling how many of his former friends had already fallen. Beyond that, even this remaining group of guards could decimate the HoluKo in an open fight. All battles between tribes were tragedies, but most were resolved more by show of strength than use of force. Those fought to the end were vicious indeed.

"I do not recognise your voice." The DanaKo chieftain stepped out from among his warriors, and SutaKe realised that he didn't recognise this man either. He recognised his rank, however: it was clearly marked by a crown of tuber stalks, woven and dyed. He was also distinctly more rotund than the other DanaKo.

"I am SutaKe, immortal leader of the HoluKo. Your warriors attacked my tribe without warning, and in the dead of night. I am here to take my revenge, but can be paid with honour in place of blood."

The chieftain raised a hand to the crowd behind him. "Cast away your arms. What he asks is fair." He turned back to SutaKe. "I am GabuKe, chieftain of the DanaKo. You are strong, SutaKe, to best my warriors, and wise to shed no more blood. However, it was foolishness to come here. You should know by now that it is not my tribesmen who are your enemy."

"Then how came your warriors to visit us with torches and not trade-goods?" SutaKe stepped forward, into the dim ring of red light. "I know who you serve, GabuKe, but the decision to serve him was your own. The steel on your soldiers' heads proves that this is so."

A flicker of something crossed GabuKe's face—more grief than firelight. "You have changed, SutaKe. Once you would have known all that happened on the island. Perhaps your village has become too remote. We did not accept Oltak's offer simply because we wanted his steel."

"Then why?" The thrill of battle was ebbing away, and once again SutaKe was tired. Once again his shoulder gave him pain. He was in no mood for these excuses.

"You know well how hard it is to hold this valley against attack. Though its great bounty supports our numbers, it is our trade that secures our safety, more than our warriors. Once, not so long ago, we were friends to all the tribes save the KasseKo, who are friends to no one. We trade our tubers freely. We trade them for things we need, like knives, and for things we merely want, like the fine stone mirrors made beyond the mountain. But those with whom we trade bring news along with their goods. News that none care to carry as far as your small village."

"What sort of news?"

GabuKe smiled, but there was pain in it. "No doubt you think Oltak's Red Turtle moored first in the bay here. No doubt you think he came to you and me alone. But this is not so. For weeks, I heard news of him from other tribes. He has been all around the island, SutaKe. His steel has bought him many friends, though he has since become a tyrant. Against the Steelmen alone, we could resist. But against all the island? No." He shook his head. "No."

SutaKe suddenly understood. "I never realised how far this had gone."

"Now you know. I am sorry for what we've done, and for all that has happened, but there could have been no other way. We must unite under Oltak or fall alone."

SutaKe had won this hopeless battle. Outnumbered and underpowered, his tribe had bested the DanaKo on their own ground. The HoluKo had been victorious, and it had won them nothing. "Is there nothing else that can be done? Together, could we not..."

"No. If nothing else, there is no time. Oltak is cunning: the last time he was here, he left Steelman spies. Search my village, if you like, but I think you'll find that they have already slipped away into the night. By morning, their master will know what has happened here. You must go to him. Go, and accept his offer as soon as you can. I will gladly give you shelter here for the night: there is no enmity between us now. No difference at all."

SutaKe gladly accepted the chieftain's hospitality. He had never expected to return to that place. He had known that it would not still be a home. But never had he thought how strange and distant it would feel, how out of place he would be. As he lay down to sleep, he thought of the HoluKo village, out beyond the valley, and it seemed no more like a home than where he was now. The presence of Oltak's ship leeched into the water. It filtered through the sand and up into the rocks and made the island itself a stranger to SutaKe. And even after the Steelmen left, he knew their influence would still remain: this was how the island would always be.

15
A VOICE AMONGST THE FLIES

The bone arrow was a great spire now, bursting from the porous rock of the mountain. It pointed, leaning, towards the DanaKo valley. There the war-club lay: its wood in splinters, its stone spikes shattered. The arrow seethed with boiling spirit-light. The broken club was dim.

"Well done, SutaKe."

He looked around for the source of the voice, and was horrified to find himself standing in a dense cloud of stinging flies. He tried to throw himself into the water of the KasseKo marsh, but found he couldn't move, couldn't even turn. He could only look towards the arrow's spire, and the smashed club of the DanaKo village. In the insects' buzzing, he recognised the spirit's voice, and so he stoically refrained from swatting at the swarming mass. "Why can't I see you?" he asked. He was beginning to suspect that this swarm was the spirit, and that their wings gave it its voice.

"Take off your mask," came the instruction.

He did as he was asked, and without the interference of its eyes began to see a pattern in the seething, six-legged bodies, though human it was not.

Twin smouldering orbs flared out from the shifting air. "I am weak, SutaKe. I could appear to you in the cave only because the warlock's bones and sinew held my spirit. A great chieftain could not see me in this form. I am too weak. I have no status. But without that mask, you are a slave as poor as I, and we can see each other, albeit dimly."

SutaKe looked around. The sky heaved with the magic of the stars. The sea heaved with all the cold life in it. And yet the place was calm. There was no danger now, no KasseKo, and he had time to take. "Who are you?" he asked first.

"Shame forbids me to speak my name. No mortal knows how weak a spirit can become without death to free it from the world. I snatch my sustenance from the mouths of flies." Ripples like arms spread through the swarm. "This, the usurping gods reduced me to, and this shall be your fate, if the Steelman has his way."

"I fear he shall. You did not tell me that he already ruled the other tribes."

"I did not know." There was genuine remorse in the spirit's buzzing voice. "But you have done well so far, SutaKe. So well. You have saved me from the mountain. You have brought your warriors to the DanaKo, and your cunning has outshone their strength."

"And it has bought me nothing!" His voice rattled the sky, shaking stardust from the churning air. "How many of my old tribe have I killed tonight? How many died for me to face the same forced trade as before?"

The spirit spoke as quietly as ever. "No more than had to die, if you are to succeed. You have taken the first step. Are you going to turn back so soon?"

"This foe is too great for any of us to face. I will not risk more lives in this futile struggle." He tied his mask back on and turned to leave. Whatever force had kept him from the marsh had since released him.

"Then you will never have her."

There was a sadness in that voice—sorrowful but sure. It struck a nerve with SutaKe. "What do you know? Perhaps Oltak will do away with the tribe-chiefs. He wants to be chieftain over all the island? Let him! Then who would there be to keep HanaRa from me?"

"You." The voice was a whisper in his ear. "You yourself. For could she love the chief who sold the tribe? Could she bear to look into your eyes? Were she in your place, she would not stop. She has been the architect of half your success already. You would not leave behind her cord: do not throw away this greater gift."

With trembling hands, SutaKe removed his mask. "Help me. Tell me what I need to do."

"The Steelmen will march tomorrow morning, and the chieftain spoke the truth about his village: there is no protection from that army there."

"Then how can we resist them? What hope do we have?"

The spirit was silent for a moment. Not even the buzzing of flies disturbed the night. "I had temples, once," it said at last. "I had temples, and people who knew my presence. They are gone now. The places of holy fire are cold."

The spirit began to weep, and each of its tiny creatures, one by one, fell to the ground like tears. SutaKe watched and said nothing, becoming aware of the ground against his side, and the night time chill of the Great Hut of the DanaKo. Only when the last insect fell did he wake, and by then it was already morning.

16
SUN

The day began in silence. The DanaKo were generous enough to share a breakfast, but though the food was good, the meal was not pleasant. The imminent surrender weighed heavy on the HoluKo, and reminded the DanaKo of their own grief. The night's wasteful battle nagged at the minds of all, and so beyond what little instruction was necessary to build up the morning fires, there was no talk between them. SutaKe was glad when, at last, the time came for his tribe to leave.

"It would be best," said GabuKe, "if your people did not take their weapons. Oltak's spies have seen our battle. If you were to go armed, the Steelmen might see that as another threat."

Before all his warriors, SutaKe stood. "If they do not bring their weapons, how will they fight?"

The chieftain of the DanaKo was stunned for a second. "What reason do they have to fight? Oltak has his victory already, my friend. Weep for it, curse it, by all means resent it, but do not challenge it. Do not throw what you still possess after what has already been lost."

"Do you know the ruins that lie above the valley, towards the coast?"

"I do."

SutaKe had been hoping for some sign of realisation in the face of GabuKe—a hint that he knew of some power in that old place—but there was none. "That place gave protection once, a long time ago. Perhaps it has some still."

"Perhaps. But even in those days when this land was closer to the In-between, magic was fickle and its price was high. Please, SutaKe, do not place your hopes in these forgotten things. If you go only to speak to Oltak—to speak and not to fight—then I can send some of my warriors. He will know them. He will listen to them. They will let you buy your safety with no more foolish risk. Please. Take what the Steelman offers: it is all that you can hope to have."

"If your warriors will not fight, you need not send them."

"Then I am sorry." GabuKe spread his arms wide. "There is nothing else that I can do."

SutaKe watched the fire for a moment. The morning light was strong, and the flame seemed to glow only dimly above its fuel. "There is one thing. Let me take some embers from your fire."

GabuKe's shoulders tightened. "Why would you need such a thing? If you use our fire to make trouble, we will suffer for it too."

"I only want to light a flame in the stone hearth of the ruins."

"And why would you want that?"

"Because..." he wondered if GabuKe would believe in the spirit. Truth be told, he wasn't sure of it himself. Another reason crossed his mind, and it was much the same: "Because I have won a battle like this once before." He sought out SanaRo amongst his tribe, then called him with a wave. "It is a tale I remember well, but...this is a task for the Storyteller to undertake."

As SanaRo approached the chieftains, the rest of the HoluKo stood and gathered round. Seeing this, GabuKe called to his people in the village and sent slaves running to fetch those out working in the fields. Thus, when all were seated by the fire, SanaRo spoke the legend to both tribes. So great were their numbers that he had to speak almost as loudly now as he had when aping the voice of Mountain in the first tale.

In ancient days when the island was new, Moon and Sun spoke. And in those ancient days, Man talked with these elements and was given great knowledge. But not all was good. As some of you already know, SutaKe tricked Mountain into stopping up his flow of ash, which was smothering the crops of the HoluKo and all the nearby tribes. He tricked him by claiming that he could hold his breath longer than Mountain, and to this day Mountain believes that the contest is still being decided. But Sun, wise Sun, saw what really happened. Sun saw SutaKe dive beneath the waves with his lungs full of air, and Sun saw him clamber from the undersea caves, leaving Mountain still staring at the place he went in.

"You are a wretch, SutaKe!" cried Sun, his voice drifting down from high above the stars. "You have played a cruel trick on my good friend! Even if you spoke to him, told the truth of what you'd done, I do not think that he would hear. You have performed an evil that cannot be undone."

"I am sorry, Sun." SutaKe spoke honestly. "Mountain may have been a friend to you, but to us he was death. His smoke pained our lungs, his fire scorched our land and his ash killed our crops. Had he listened to our earnest pleas, I would not have had to stop up his ears with my falsehood."

An ugly shadow passed across the face of Sun. "The hubris of you mortals knows no bounds! Do you think it is your right to say how we great elements can use our power? I saw that Mountain's ash blighted your crops. I am not as blind as you have made him deaf! But though Mountain's strength brought you harm, mine gives life! You thought to end his influence upon the island? Then I shall end mine too." And like a rushlight being snuffed, Sun's face vanished from the sky.

Had Moon not still cast forth her distant glow, the island would have torn itself apart. Great was the fear of the HoluKo, and even all the creatures of the forest, for never before had Sun held back his light. This was the first night the island ever saw, and none has brought such terror since. But SutaKe realised that Sun was still there, only hiding in his darkness, and so he spoke.

"Sun!" SutaKe shouted to the heavens. "This rage of yours shows that you are just as vain as Mountain. See sense now, and I will not be forced to use my power to bend you to my will, as I did your friend."

"Power?" From the great darkness, Sun spoke. "You have no power, pitiful thing. Your victory over Mountain was won with a trick—a poor trick at that—and I shall not be so easily overthrown. Nothing you can say will make me give you back my light.

"I have no need of your light, sky-lantern! We basked in your warmth for convenience, and not for any need. Light and heat, our small fires give both, and with a greater fire you shall be replaced! Do you hear that, star-spark? You are worth less to us than a lump of wood upon the sand. Man's beacon shall light the land where Sun once shone."

"Do it, then." Blazing meteors tumbled from Sun's dim mouth, but gave off little light. "Make your fire, and I'll have nothing more to do with you."

"You'll regret those words," said SutaKe. "Our flames are hotter than your light. You shall not merely be replaced: you shall be outshone. In years to come, my people shall look up at your dim space in the sky and ask: 'What is that?' They shall ask, and I will tell them: 'That is just a smudge upon the heavens, far away. Perhaps in time the rain will wash it from the sky.' You shall not merely be replaced, Sun: you shall be forgotten."

The power held by Sun was great indeed, and truly no mere fire could replace it. But while SutaKe knew this, Sun did not. Sun had often looked down upon Man's fire with a faint trembling of fear. Man could not construct another Mountain, nor forge the spirit-light of Moon, but in those little flames Sun saw himself. Still, Sun was angry for his lost friend, and when he spoke his voice was strong. "So be it, mortal. You will fail and your crops will die, and still I shall not shine: not even for the pleasure of bleaching your bones." But inwardly he trembled still.

Sun was right to tremble, for SutaKe's cunning worked stronger now even than it had with Mountain. He went to find the Stoneman of the HoluKo and, finding him, ordered that a great quantity of smooth, flat obsidian be gathered together. In their fear, the HoluKo worked quickly, and the material was quarried before the sunless ground had even cooled.

SutaKe instructed the Stoneman not to chip apart the stones, as he would do for tools, but to take sand and straw and polish their flat sides to a flawless sheen. While the Stoneman worked, the other members of the tribe set about collecting great heaps of firewood. Had Sun seen these two tasks performed, he would have been suspicious. But without light, even Sun was blind, and so the tasks remained unseen.

At last, with wood and polished stones all set together, SutaKe put his cunning plan in place. The stones he had set out—all flat side up—in a great circle on clear ground. Like a pool on a windless night, this surface caught and threw back any light that touched it. Upon this he placed a stand for the fire, as for a bright beacon on a hill. Upon this stand, the wood was set, so that the great heat of the flames would not crack the glass. At last, SutaKe called out his challenge.

"Sun!" he shouted. "In the light of this torch, you see the pyre with which we shall replace you. See how much wood it holds? See the sap-rich twigs and heavy logs? Your primeval flame cannot burn brighter than this marvel made by Man. I give you one last chance. Cast away your bitter feelings, and we will once again live by your inferior light."

Sun trembled, but knew that in the dark it could not be seen. Breathing calmly for a minute, he made his voice defiant once again. "No more talk, trickster. Set fire to your feeble work. Burn your little rushlight reeds. You'll strip the island bare before your light could rival half of mine." But inwardly he quaked.

SutaKe held the torch to his great beacon, and at once the flame began to gnaw. Though his speech to Sun had been a hollow boast, *there was yet truth in it. Never since has such a fire blazed as that, the flame of Man's first night. Huge glowing boughs tumbled to the earth, shattering into white-hot coals. Sparks the size of spearheads rose, taunting the stars with their brightness. And a smoke went up hotter than any that Mountain had ever cast forth.*

Sun was confident the fire burned not as bright as he had done himself. Yet how could he be sure? The pressing darkness of that first night had robbed his mind of even memories of light. And would not Man's mind be the same? Sun began to fret. He did not want to be forgotten! He would, he decided, only match SutaKe's pyre. He would glow as bright only, and no brighter, so that should the fire sputter and die, Man's crops should still fail. And if it never dimmed, then Sun at least would be remembered. With this thought in mind, Sun began to shine once more.

As Sun's light fell across the land, his confidence grew. Yes, he thought. Yes, the chieftain's boast had been no cause for fear. Even such a fire as that could not light the whole island. Not like Sun. And yet...that one spot, the flame itself, seemed brighter even than before. Sun choked in surprise, sending out a cloud of smoke to swirl among the stars. The light of this fire was brighter than his own! Terrified that he would not even be remembered, Sun burned brighter, matching himself against the flame. Yet every time he increased his light, the fire grew brighter too. Soon, Sun burned as bright as ever, and still the flame outshone.

Sun began to panic. Even with the island lit as brightly as it had ever been, that one glimmer—the flame of Man—was stronger than the light of Sun, and cast its mocking glare into Sun's eyes. In one last, desperate effort, Sun drew deep a breath and blew upon himself, as Man blows upon an ember. But even as Sun's breath brightened his flames, the fire of Man shone still more brightly. And so Sun blew for evermore, puffing and staring at the fire Man had built to replace him. But never could Sun's light outshine that flame, and out of shame, never does he speak.

But Sun, like Mountain, had been deceived. SutaKe's bright fire had burnt out even before Sun began to blow: the light he saw shining up from the island was his own, reflected in the great mosaic mirror

SutaKe had built beneath his flame. So while Mountain was tricked into withholding his deathly ash, Sun was made to give more warmth even than before, so that the crops of Man would flourish in his light. SutaKe boasted of this to the HoluKo, who rejoiced, but one who listened to his speech was still not pleased. Moon, lonely Moon, had seen what happened, and indeed saw more than Man. For this reason, Moon came down to speak.

"SutaKe," said Moon. "With cruel tricks have you deceived both my friends. First Mountain, who forged the ground beneath your feet, and now Sun, who sought only vengeance for your first misdeed. Neither now can speak. Your crimes have indeed grown great, and someday I too must mete out a punishment. But for now, your cunning has its own reward. Look how Sun's panicked breath moves him through the sky!"

SutaKe looked up just in time to see Sun dart down below the sea—the first time this had ever happened—and all the HoluKo were too shocked even to be afraid. Moon's light washed over all, and the mirror put forth no reflection.

"Sun will return," Moon explained. "In his accidental voyage, he shall circle the island again and again, heedless of his course, rising and setting each and every day. You have set that orb in motion, SutaKe, and not even I can stop it. Nor would I try. My friend burns twice as brightly as before, but you shall have his light for only half the time. Such is the way of the things Man makes: you have created Day, SutaKe, but with it you have crafted Night."

And so it came to be that, while SutaKe won back the light of Sun, fire too would have its part to play. For new-created Night brought cold and dark, and man-made Suns alone must hold them back.

17
THE STORM OF ARROWS

SutaKe had forgotten that the second tale had such a sombre ending, and almost wished that SanaRo had thought to tell it differently to the DanaKo. But though one story may mean many things, the words at least must stay the same, and so SutaKe made no attempt to change the tale that had been told.

He turned to face GabuKe once again. "If such a ploy can best the sun, might it not be the same with the Steelmen, who are not as strong?"

"It is not their strength that you should fear," GabuKe replied. "The Steelmen are not so strong, and most have shown no cunning greater than our own. But Oltak, their leader, has formed a great and winding plan, and wins battles that he does not fight."

"Then make him fight! In truth, I cannot say what good the fire may bring. But you know as I do that if Oltak's army marches uncontested, no good will come. Only give me embers, and if all fails, Oltak will never know."

GabuKe thought seriously. "Very well." Under his

instruction, two warriors of the DanaKo brought a hollow log, stuffed with grass and clay, and packaged embers for SutaKe to carry. When the time came, those hot coals would make a new flame in an instant, and SutaKe knew how greatly that was needed. Having waited for SanaRo's story, he felt sure the Steelmen would already be on their way.

Halfway down the valley did the HoluKo march. All along the river, SutaKe looked for some place to make a stand, some place where good ground would strip good steel of its advantage. But the valley sides were gentle and the cover was poor. Any place that would weaken the Steelmen would weaken the HoluKo too, and in any place the tribesmen could hold strong, the Steelmen too would find new strength. The ruins, he discovered, were the only place where the HoluKo could hope to hold their ground: magic or no magic.

Set above a curious slope of rock—spilled forth by the mountain in forgotten times—the temple slept. SutaKe approached it from upstream, climbing the valley side where it was not so steep. The Steelmen, he knew, would face a harder climb coming up from the coast, or would have to circle round. This was good, but alone it was not enough to make up for their strength in steel. For a moment then, he hated GabuKe—too afraid to lend the weapons for which he had sold his tribe—but this passed. Their chances of success were slim enough. Those new swords would not be worth the risk of bringing punishment upon the DanaKo, and his family among them. Putting these thoughts out of his mind, SutaKe looked once more about the ruins.

There, in the centre, was the place for fire. A grand dish set upon a stout pillar, time's rough fingers had worn its carvings down to naught. Around the edge of the raised stone floor, further pillars stood and some reclined. Whatever roof they had once held—if any roof had ever been—had either burned or rotted in days gone by. He looked up to the sky, the sun already halfway to its greatest height. It would be easy, he thought, if this foe could be threatened with its own reflection, but it was not to be. The Steelmen carried mirrors in their hands and on their heads and, looking from this high place into the valley below, he could see them glinting in the light.

"Set the fire!" cried SutaKe. "Find wood and straw to feed the dish, and have the embers ready!"

With many hands, and the help of the hot embers, the fire leapt up quickly. But this swift success was not enough. When SutaKe looked down into the valley, he saw the Steelmen directly below, oblivious to the pale smoke. They had not seen the HoluKo as they approached, and in their careless march—spears used as walking staves, shields slung over backs—he saw how pitiful this struggle was. The blazing altar would be no help. This battle was theirs alone to fight, and looking at the ordered mass below, he saw that it was not one they could win. But he had come too far to give up now.

"More wood!" he called. "More wood!"

In the valley down below, the Steelmen heard. They looked up at the leaning ruins and saw the smoke—thick and black now the fire had grown, and the HoluKo had brought green wood to feed the flames. As one square creature, clothed in scales, the Steelmen turned.

Arrows hurtled through the air, thudding into flesh and shattering against stone. One struck the fire, tipping a glowing log down to the floor, but still no spirit rose from the altar. Marching along with the shield-wearing warriors, SutaKe had not seen the archers in the ranks of the Steelmen.

"Come forward, archers! But all others, find shelter." Peering from around one of the great pillars, he watched the enemy's approach.

The battle was brutal for one side alone. Even with the

benefit of higher ground, the bows of the HoluKo could not match those of the Steelmen, whose weapons were of marvellous construction. They held their bows not with their hands, but against a stout staff, which drew and held the string. At some command of the archer's grasp, the bow would whip back, letting fly its lethal dart. Those arrows were shorter than those used by the HoluKo, but the bows of the Steelmen held much greater force. So powerful were those bows that the Steelmen had to stoop and draw them with both hands—one foot pinning the weapon to the ground. A steel arrowhead struck the pillar by SutaKe's face, and he felt gravel spit against his mask. Crouching low, he continued to watch.

The warriors of the Steelmen—those armed with sword or spear—were useful even while their weapons weren't. Marching forth as one dense block, they held their shields out in front, overlapping and interlocking so that no arrow could pass through. Over this living wall, their strange archers took their shots, and behind the archers came more spearmen still, ready to replace the few that fell. This strong defence made them slow, but SutaKe could see they had no need to hurry. The archers who had so easily overpowered the DanaKo were little good here, and his outnumbered warriors had no hope. SutaKe looked to the fire one last time, hoping beyond hope that the spirit would arrive.

"SutaKe!" NaruKa hurried over, trying to stay in the poor shelter of a toppled pillar. "We cannot hold this ground. There are too many. They are too well armed. Let us choose a better battle on some different day."

"There will be no better days! If we..."

A steel-tipped arrow quivered between NaruKa's ribs. The warrior fell but did not scream. SutaKe stared at the body, then down along the hillside. The creature of wood and metal lumbered closer on its many shoe-clad feet. His archers had faced it and failed, and his warriors would stand no chance, but SutaKe did not call the retreat. Oltak would not trade with the HoluKo now. They had nowhere to run.

"I'm sorry, NaruKa." SutaKe remembered the meeting in the Great Hut, days ago. "You would have taken the Steelman's offer. If we had done as you wanted, this would never have happened." Crouching ready behind the fallen pillar, he waited for the Steelmen to come within reach of his spear. There was not much space to shelter there, and SutaKe found he had to press in close behind the stone to avoid the arrows launched up from the hillside. Several struck the rock in quick succession, and he realised that the archers could see his spearhead wavering above the pillar where he hid. Hastily, he tucked the weapon down into the crevice between pillar and floor.

It was only when spear and pillar came together that he realised the importance of this place. It had not been the fire at all.

Heedless of the arrows flying through the air, SutaKe stood. He wedged his spear beneath the pillar and began to push, leaning all his weight on the stout shaft. Out in the open, exposed at the very edge of the hill, all eyes were upon him, and all saw what they had to do. Though SutaKe's strength alone was not enough, others quickly came to add their own, testing clubs, bows, bare hands against the pillar's weight. And in one smooth motion, it began to fall.

The little drop from floor to hillside gave it all the force it needed to make its journey. Seeing the great thing bearing down upon them, the Steelmen broke. Some fell forwards to the ground, faces buried in the shallow loam. Others darted sideways, out of the pillar's bounding path. A handful tore away down the hillside, fleeing blindly. Still more had no time to move at all. And whatever that rock pillar touched, it obliterated. Steel armour bent like leaves beneath its blows, and thoughtless stone could fear no steel spears. Seeing the devastation that thing caused, SutaKe was almost sorry he had unleashed it, but this feeling faded when he saw how the survivors spaced themselves and charged. The Steelmen had not been merely well equipped: they were fierce warriors, and their loss had caused in them more hate than fear.

But the pillar had done its terrible work. Those with shields had been the hardest hit, and without the protection of rank and form the arbalesters quickly fell to the arrows of the HoluKo. The remaining warriors made their charge against the temple grounds, and here the battle at last was fought. KanaKa's new-mended spear was more vicious even than before, wreathed around with amulets of thorns, and its old stone head found weakness in ten newer shirts of steel.

The centre of the fight stood motionless—an unyielding line of Steelman shield against HoluKo spear—but at the edges all was movement. The few Steelmen still with bows made a run for the trees at the top of the valley, while skirmishers with swords struggled to surround the temple. Checking their progress, SutaKe turned his head to see BaraKa cleave a helmet clean in two, the sheer force of his sword letting glass trump steel. The Steelmen were brave—presented with this line of hard-set faces, no one could deny it—but their assault did not last long. Winning no purchase on the temple floor, they turned and hurried back along the valley, where the river flowed to the sea, for there the Red Turtle waited. Of those who had marched upon the ruins, a full two thirds would never leave.

But though this marked the first victory against the Steelmen themselves, there was little cause to celebrate. Many besides NaruKa had fallen in the storm of arrows. Still more had been wounded in the battle-line. Yes, the hopeless fight had been won once more, but this time the price had been too great. Another such victory would doom them all.

BaraKa clambered back up to the temple floor. "What should we do now, SutaKe?"

SutaKe looked around at the wounded left in the ruins, and the wreckage on the hillside. "Rest here," he said. "Let the fire burn down, then refill the log. We will take back GabuKe's coals." SutaKe watched the blaze. Again the spirit's words had bought them a new day, but this time he knew a night must follow, and flame alone could never hold it back.

18
A FACELESS FRIEND

There were drums and flutes playing when the HoluKo returned to the village in the valley, but SutaKe knew that they sounded their song for tradition alone. If Oltak's power extended as far across the island as GabuKe had claimed, this small victory could not loosen its hold. And yet, as SanaRo tipped the embers back onto the fire, and the warriors laid out their captured steel, there was a sense that this jubilation was genuine, and that the battle had not been in vain.

"Well, done, my friend!" GabuKe clapped him on the back. "Well done!"

SutaKe spoke quietly. "If you had seen the battle, I think you would not be so pleased."

"But I did see it." GabuKe smiled. "Only, not in person. I sent a runner after you—I hope you will forgive me—and he has told me all that happened. Not all the warriors of the DanaKo could have turned back such a force as you have faced today."

"But surely more will come. The trick we used today will

not work twice."

"But once, I think, will be enough. How many bodies do you think the Red Turtle can hold?"

SutaKe did not know. He had heard that the ships of the Steelmen could be huge—so huge that their single hulls had no need of outriggers—and had always imagined something like a village on the waves. But GabuKe's face suggested that this was not so.

"My runner once made a journey to Oltak's camp. He saw there the trader's entire retinue, and that, my friend, is what you faced today. Oltak has all the tribes to the South—hundreds of warriors from our local shores—but he has lost the army that he brought by sea. Without that, I think, those he once threatened will now serve our cause better than his."

SutaKe had never thought of this. One by one, the Steelman had brought the tribes to serve his will. But without warriors truly loyal to his cause, those united under him would be just as easily united against him. "Do you think they could be swayed?"

"It is difficult to say. Many of the smaller tribes would take any chance to overthrow this merchant tyrant. But you must know that not all his trades were bad. Those chieftains that he came to first, those whose favour he truly had to win...these see him as a friend. A powerful friend. A friend they would not care to lose. It is not only Oltak's shattered army that we face, but these, his puppet-chiefs."

"However many allies we may find, that battle will be fierce indeed."

"Sadly, yes. And still I can't be sure it can be won. But I will send out traders of my own, to take good gifts to neighbouring tribes and see if we can't secure their allegiance to our cause. But know this: whether I find success or failure here, the DanaKo are friends to you, so neither tribe must fight alone. Please, stay one more night. Before we think ahead to new battles, let us feast to celebrate this one now passed." He patted his belly, smiling around at the reconciled tribes.

"Thank you," said SutaKe, "but we must return to our own place. The others will be worried, and in these violent times it does not do to keep the warriors away too long."

The journey back to the HoluKo village did not seem as taxing as it had done before, but nevertheless SutaKe was glad when they finally arrived. Twice now he had set out for a battle from which he had not expected to return. Even that, he considered, had not been enough to free the HoluKo from the prospect of yet another struggle.

Shortly before they reached the village, HanaRa hurried to meet the group of returning warriors. The look on her face made SutaKe afraid she was bringing horrible news. However, she offered the chieftain only a glance: whatever concerns she had were too small for SutaKe. Crying, she spoke to KanaKa instead: "I'm glad you came back. However the battle went, that's all that matters to me." It was only then that SutaKe realised how sorry his small party must have looked. The joy of their recent victories could not outshine the dull weariness caused by hard battle and long walk.

KanaKa, laughing, took hold of HanaRa's arms. "What? Are these tears? I thought you had more faith in me! No doubt your mother's been fretting too, though she knows I've faced worse foes than this."

HanaRa tried to laugh, too, but it was plain that she was still upset. "You were gone a long time."

"Because we won two battles. It wouldn't take nearly so long to lose one."

KanaKa told HanaRa of the DanaKo and the army of the Steelmen, and SutaKe left them walking behind as he made his way along the short path back to the village. When he arrived, he found that the slaves had already begun to feed the fire. TakuMe—one of SutaKe's own—was amongst them, though he had fought alongside the warriors who now sat exhausted in the dust. SutaKe quietly walked over and gave him his freedom. That evening, many slaves would be made free, and many free men named warriors. But when HanaRa at last returned with her father, he could see that she did not share entirely in the celebrations of the tribe.

"Oltak is a cunning enemy," she said. "Surely he will have thought that this could happen? You said that he had spies amongst the DanaKo."

"Spies who fled the moment we came near. Without the threat of that steel army, the other tribes will have little reason not to take our side. The DanaKo have many friends amongst the chiefs."

"Perhaps. I hope so, at least."

HanaRa, as always, had thought of danger no one else had seen. But in the happy light of the village fire, as families were reunited, it was hard to hold on to such solemn thoughts, and SutaKe did not care to try. Sitting on a stout log close to the blaze, the hot light bleached away the day's cold toil. But almost too slowly for him to notice, a faint buzzing became audible over the crackling of wood in flame. And as the buzzing grew, the voices of the HoluKo began to die away. SutaKe felt a hand upon his shoulder.

"Once more you have done well," the spirit said. "The people's faith in you has strengthened me. Soon I shall be able to step beyond the In-between, and lend my power to your cause. But for now, you must make do with what I see through the thin reed-wall of the world."

SutaKe unfastened the straps of his mask and looked up at the spirit, standing behind him. It had a solid shape now, and he was surprised to see that it was human. The limbs had all the right proportions, and the skin held even little hairs, like any member of any tribe. Only the face remained unwhole: the eyes sat like heated moons, suspended in the void of night, and here was where the buzzing had its heart.

The sight was unsettling, but compared to Oltak's false-kind face, its truthful horror was almost welcome.

"Thank you for telling of the temple," SutaKe said. "The battle was costly, but without your words it could not have been won. And things are better now. The DanaKo are allies once again, and with their strength and size, other tribes will surely join with us in time."

"Others, yes..." there was human feeling in the spirit's doubt. "Others, but not enough. You have won your ally well, but do not trust in him too much. The chieftain of the DanaKo is a spear shaft, broken and renewed. For simple work, it is enough—for throwing in a hunt, or spearing fish—but take it into battle and you will find it more an enemy than a friend. You can never be sure that the part once broken will not break again, and drive its jagged end into your chest." The spirit cast a hand over the fire, and in the flames SutaKe saw the DanaKo raiding the village once again, this time in full force. GabuKe was amongst them.

He shuddered. "What must I do?"

"Do not trouble yourself over what I have shown." Stirring the embers with a stick, the spirit scrubbed the image from the flame. "This represents only a thing that might happen, and the chieftain of the DanaKo might yet be a useful ally. Only, do not put on him too great a strain. There are other events I see that must be, and that nothing can prevent."

Faintly, SutaKe heard the tribe around him moving and talking, but when he looked about the fire all were still: glowing shadows of their solid selves. "What are these things you see?"

"It is this: GabuKe will fail. Your friend has told you that he will seek out allies, and that he will bring them to your cause. This was not a lie—he will find many warriors—but what he does is not enough. You must have more. All around the island, the chieftains bowed to the merchant, but you must have warriors who remained unbought."

"But if all the island serves the merchant, who else is there?"

The mouthless face seemed to smile. "Not all the island, SutaKe. Only all around it. One tribe remains. One in the centre. One that can never be bought."

"Who?"

"You know them already. You know them well by now."

As the dream ended, a hissing chant went up about the fire. But when SutaKe woke fully, he found that it was only a sudden wind in the trees, drawing him back from the In-between. He had learned to trust the spirit by now—its words, and not his cunning, had led the tribe so far—but even so he doubted its advice. The tribe in the centre, the tribe that remained, the tribe that could never be bought: this tribe was the KasseKo, and they were an enemy more terrible even than the Steelmen.

19
VOICE OF PEARL

For days, SutaKe wondered how he could make an ally of the KasseKo, and if such a thing was even possible. He considered that the spirit might not have meant for him to speak to them, but instead only to guide them into a position where they would be useful to his cause. The KasseKo were like a woodland fire, violent and uncontrollable. They might be lured to the site of a battle, or perhaps some clever trick could be used to force the puppet-chiefs to brave the lands around the mountain. But SutaKe remembered well the spirit's words, and he knew that this was not its will. He would win the service of the KasseKo, or he would lose his tribe.

At first, SutaKe hoped that he would be visited by the spirit once again, that there was further truth he could be told. But this too felt somehow wrong. The spirit, like the sun, was moved by forces from beyond the world. It obeyed these unseen rules and, once its time for speech had passed, it would not come again until the stars once more held its fate in harmony with his. Soon its power would permit it to do more, but until then SutaKe knew he would have to do with what little it had lent. He slept two nights before embarking on his journey to the mountain. He would have slept for more, but for the risk that soon the Steelman might make his move.

The morning after those two nights, SutaKe was prepared to leave. But, even after saying his goodbyes, even after taking up his spear, he knew that there was something he had missed. The more he thought about his task, the more he realised that this was something he could not do alone.

"SanaRo?" He found the craftsman in front of his workshop hut, chipping tiny flakes of glass from the blunt edge of a spearhead.

"Yes?"

"There is something I must ask you to do, but it is a dangerous thing. If you refuse, I will not ask again."

"You want me to go with you to the KasseKo."

"Yes."

SanaRo sighed. "As Stoneman of the tribe, I should refuse. Without me here, the blades of the HoluKo would be blunt, and arrows would go headless. But as Storyteller, I must go. It is one of my tasks. It is mine, in fact, more than it is yours. It has always been the Storyteller who unites two tribes."

"Even so, there would be no dishonour in staying."

"Perhaps not, but..." SanaRo set down his tools. "SutaKe, do you have a task for me? Do you truly need a Storyteller, or would any of your warriors do?"

"It must be the Storyteller."

"Then I will go." He looked up at the low sun. "But one tale remains to be told here. I will start now, so as not to keep you." He stood, starting towards the morning fire.

"Wait."

SanaRo stopped.

"The final tale. I do not remember it well...at least, not

as well as I used to." He had been playing the part of SutaKe for so long that he had begun to make new mistakes. It was hard now to remember that his history was not the hero's own. "If this is the tale of the wager with Moon—the gift-giving contest—then it must wait to be told. It is not the HoluKo who must hear it this time."

"Are you sure?" SanaRo paused. "That tale could be told twice. It would not do to leave here and risk having the story remain unfinished."

For a moment, SutaKe almost yielded. The third tale was not the happiest, but it was the most significant. And though it was not the most honest, it spoke the most truth. There was every chance that, if he now led SanaRo to the KasseKo, the tales of Mountain and Sun would forever remain incomplete. But again there was a sense that anything else would be improper. Fate was weaving its own narrative, and it would not stand to be interrupted by the same tale twice. "I am sure," he said.

The journey to the mountain was now so familiar that it did not seem so long. But with SanaRo trudging through the forest behind him, SutaKe found the way more lonely, and not less. Here in the homeland of the KasseKo, they could not risk the noise of speaking. More than once, they had to steer away from the sound of rattles and hunting chants, but no party came as close as the one SutaKe had encountered along the stream. It was by that route they travelled, though, having not already begun the longer journey through the quarry.

SutaKe was so accustomed to the withered heads in the mountain cave that he was almost surprised to see SanaRo hesitate.

"Those are talismans," SutaKe explained. "They were made to honour the warlock."

"And he was happy to have been given them?"

"It seemed so, yes."

SutaKe noticed that the body of the KasseKo tribesman

had been removed, as had the items shattered during their brief struggle. RanaZo, too, was no longer sitting...but now it was SutaKe's turn to be unsettled. Placed neatly in the centre of the stone table, wand gripped between its pointed teeth, was the warlock's boiled skull. SutaKe fiercely hoped this was a token of reverence among the KasseKo. If not, what he was about to do would be foolish indeed.

Exactly where RanaZo had left it—within easy reach of the seating place behind the table—was the conch, pink and glossy in the cave-door's light. He studied it for a minute, looking for any trick or trap the shell might hold.

"May I?" SanaRo held out a hand.

Since SutaKe's mask would not allow him to blow— even if he had known what to do—he passed the conch to SanaRo, and on only the third or fourth attempt, the Storyteller produced a great resounding blast, the noise further amplified by the walls of the cave. Even his penultimate try, SutaKe thought, may have been clear enough to carry its message to the KasseKo.

"And now we simply wait for them to come?"

"It's the only way." SutaKe shrugged. "We need to talk with them. If they had found us in the forest...if we hadn't made it clear that we had come to speak..." SanaRo would surely understand. "We need these people."

"I have heard the KasseKo called many things. 'People' has never been one of them."

The two sat down to wait, but they almost needn't have bothered. The footsteps at the entrance came so quickly that SutaKe suspected that he and SanaRo might have been followed. The man who appeared in the doorway was an archer, much the same as the one he had encountered here before. But while that man had come with club raised, this one came with bow drawn, and remained outside the cave. There was no way of reaching him with sword or spear— not before he loosed that arrow—and so SanaRo and SutaKe remained perfectly still, sitting and waiting.

"Who are you?" The bow remained as taught as ever. "Tell me. Why do you speak with Voice of Pearl?"

"To bring a message: one that I will give only to your chieftain."

The arrow made a sudden lunge forwards, causing SutaKe to flinch, but the archer had only let the bow relax, holding the string back with his hand. He gestured to somebody outside the cave. SutaKe could hear talking: there must have been at least two others.

"The KasseKo follow no false chief. Only Tribe-mother, Tribe-father. This is the proper way."

"Then my message must be for them."

In hushed tones, the archer spoke with someone just out of sight, by the cave entrance. SutaKe could not make out the whole conversation, but he heard the reply: "Bones that walk need not be carried."

It was not the most auspicious start to the meeting with the tribe, but SutaKe felt lucky nonetheless. Offering no resistance, he and SanaRo left the cave with the people who had come to find them. The KasseKo had, SutaKe knew, carried messages for RanaZo. They were not without words. But never before then, he thought, had anyone but the warlock heard them speak on their own land.

"I am KodaRo," said the archer, quite unexpectedly.

"We are SutaKe and SanaRo." SutaKe looked ahead at the other KasseKo who had come. All carried spiked clubs or short, wide-bladed spears. "What are the names of the others?"

"They will not speak to you," KodaRo explained. "Nobody wants to waste their magic talking to outsiders."

"Then it is very kind of you to do so."

"I didn't want to either, but I have a great deal to spare." Proudly, KodaRo lifted an amulet from his belt. Eleven dry fingers hung from it in a grisly cluster. SutaKe thought he might have seen the thing before.

The KasseKo village—if village it could be called—lay

on a flat patch of grassland at the foot of the mountain, not far from the marsh. They had no proper huts, instead taking shelter under canopies of boar hides, set at an angle to shed the rain and hemmed about by bundles of reeds. The whole place had a look that suggested it could be taken up and moved at any time. This would partly explain why no tribe had ever launched a raid against it in retaliation for past battles. But though the dwellings seemed temporary, always new, there were old relics strewn about. As the party escorting SutaKe entered the village—through a standing gateway hung with bones—each man said an incomprehensible prayer, touching the long snout of a crocodile skull as they passed. SutaKe wasn't sure whether or not to do the same, but fortunately KodaRo dispelled all doubt.

"This is our magic," he said, after completing his prayer. "It is ours alone." So SutaKe and SanaRo stepped through without ceremony.

However strange the customs of the KasseKo, and however brutish its people, they had one thing in common with all the other tribes: the fire. As always, it was in the centre of the village and, as always, it was the centre of all that happened there. But still SutaKe was surprised to find that there was no Great Hut here: not even a tent to serve its purpose. The Tribe-mother and Tribe-father—for SutaKe was sure it was these he saw—sat in the dirt before the fire with their backs to the flames.

Both wore heaps of amulets and great clusters of carved bones, and at their belts hung heavy talismans engraved with strange designs. Tribe-father wore a mask—almost a helmet—crafted from two skulls. His right eye peered out from the right skull's left, and his left eye from the left skull's right, so that his two living eyes were flanked by two dead sockets. His nose sat square between the skulls, looking somewhat out of place. He was, SutaKe noted, also this tribe's Stoneman, or the KasseKo equivalent. He had the tools to hand and his place by the fire—though not marked out in any meaningful way—was littered with the fragments of his work.

Tribe-mother wore nothing on her face, but her ears and nose held shell ornaments more impressive than anything even the DanaKo could trade for. Since the KasseKo never ventured to the coast, SutaKe assumed that these must have been won in battle. She looked to KodaRo, but did not speak, waiting instead for him to give his news.

"Tribe-mother," said KodaRo. "While out hunting, we heard Voice of Pearl, though all now know that RanaZo is dead. We found these two in his cave. The one in the mask is SutaKe, a chieftain of the coast. He claims to have a message you must hear."

"I very much doubt that there is any news worth hearing from the coast." Tribe-father rubbed at a small stone cut on his finger. "We have the island's heart. What goes on around its outskirts is of no concern to us, especially now that RanaZo no longer watches from the sacred cave." He looked to Tribe-mother, waiting to hear her speak.

"Nevertheless," she said, "you were right to bring him. I will hear this message. Regardless of its importance, the bones of chieftains hold strong magic, and this is always welcome."

SutaKe hoped his plan would work. The consequences of failure did not bear thinking about: those whose bodies became amulets for the KasseKo would never reach the white island as spirits. "I will give you my message," he said, "and I promise it is important. Were it not, you know I would never have dared to bring it."

"This is true." Tribe-mother looked to Tribe-father, and he nodded.

"Yet," continued SutaKe, "it is the custom among my people, when we meet new friends for the first time, to exchange gifts of equal value."

"That is not the custom here." There was a harsh edge

to Tribe-father's voice. "My people do not care for the powerless trinkets the coast-tribes trade. No item you can give would have value in our eyes, and so our gift to you is nothing."

"In light of this," added Tribe-mother, not unkindly, "it is not necessary that you give your gift to us. The message, however, we will hear."

SutaKe turned his attention to Tribe-father alone. "My gift to you is not an item," he explained, "and I think you will find worth in it. My gift is a tale from my tribe. A good tale, and one that I do not think has been shared before."

The start of a snarl crossed Tribe-father's face below the mask, but Tribe-mother stopped his speech before it began, placing a hand gently upon his arm. "It has been a long time since we heard a new tale. This is a kind gift indeed, and one I at least would be willing to return."

"I am very glad to hear that." SutaKe did not exaggerate. "SanaRo will tell the tale. He is the Storyteller of the HoluKo, and I brought him for this purpose. You must let him leave when his story is done."

"We must trade gifts? We must let this intruder leave?" Tribe-father stood, whipping a vicious stone blade from his belt as he did so. "Impose any more of your customs on us, foreigner, and I will show you some of ours!"

SanaRo stepped forwards, placing a hand in front of SutaKe. "We did not mean to abuse your patience. My chief is kind to ask this guarantee, but I will tell the tale without it. Let its merit speak for us both."

20

MOON

The whole tribe of the KasseKo began to gather round—all rattling bones and low whispers—but SanaRo did not let this distract him. He was a good Storyteller, and he began, as always, in the proper way.

In ancient days when the island was new, Moon spoke. Mountain and Sun once spoke too, but both threatened Man and so SutaKe tricked them into silence.

SutaKe looked about him at the tribe. The KasseKo would know nothing of this tale, let alone the two that had come before. But despite this, they still seemed interested: many had set themselves down to sit, and so seemed eager to hear the whole thing.

From these elements, then, Man was safe. But not all was good. Moon had grown lonely without her companions to talk to, and had made known her intention to punish Man for SutaKe's deception.

Moon waited almost a year before laying down her punishment— for Moon was clever, and not unkind—but as her loneliness grew only greater, and as her grief had grown no less, the penalty she settled on for Man was grave indeed.

SutaKe noted that even the KasseKo still standing seemed to have let themselves become absorbed in the tale—thin, blank faces staring at the speaker—and so allowed himself to do the same.

"SutaKe," Moon greeted Man, "and all the HoluKo. You know well how your tricks have pained me. Though my friends, Sun and Mountain, are still beside me, they do not speak. Their company no longer brings me joy. You know well also that, when your people die, they come to me. They walk about upon my shores, and I ensure that there is food, water and shelter enough for all. You can see this, and you can speak to them, whenever you care to look upon me in the sky."

The HoluKo were silent. Long had they been expecting Moon to deal out her punishment, and always had they known that it would be severe. But whatever Moon dictated now was sure to be terrible, since it involved the spirits on her shores.

"It occurs to me," continued Moon, "that these people that you loved and lost are not so different to you than Sun and Mountain were to me. It is fitting, then, that your pain should be the same as mine. I intend to lift myself high into the heavens, so that you can never see or speak to me again. Death now shall hold greater horror even than before, since the spirits of your fallen ones shall not be seen again."

The HoluKo began to weep. This punishment was harsh indeed, and all would feel it hard to bear. Seeing his people so moved, SutaKe spoke.

"Moon," he called up to the sky. "It is right that you should have some vengeance. I cannot deny that I have wronged you. But I did so only to save my people. I did so only because there was no other way. And though I see that I have harmed you with my deeds, not once did I wish to quarrel with you. Because of this, I think your punishment too cruel. Let me have some opportunity to wash my crimes away, and thus avoid it."

"SutaKe," Moon spoke down. "My fellow elements thought Man grew bold. That his great pride had grown beyond his little power. But I remained apart and watched while they ran to crush you. I see in you no hubris to abhor: your pride has grown, but not out of proportion to

your power. And so I look on you not with disgust, but fear."

"But still we could be friends, Moon. If only you would forget how we have wronged you, would put off your punishment, you would have no need to fear."

Moon shed stars as tears, and all the HoluKo could see her grief was true. "No," *she said.* "Deception has robbed me of my friends, so honest must I be with you. It is not only for your punishment that I intend to drift away, but for my own protection. SutaKe, each element that has drawn within your grasp, you have seized and subdued. Mountain does your will, and does not speak. Sun does your will, and does not speak. I have little doubt that, were I to quarrel with you further, I would come to share their fate."*

"But what if..."

"You propose a wager?" Moon smiled. "I know how that tale would end, SutaKe. I have heard it twice before. Should you issue any challenge, I must refuse. I have no wish to put my power within your grasp, and not merely because I fear you now. You have harnessed the power of Mountain and Sun already. Were you to have mine too, were you to wield all three elements, you would become a god."*

"And why should that worry you so?" Something in Moon's voice made SutaKe forget his grief. "I conquered Mountain only because his callousness would have killed us. I conquered Sun only because he made thoughtless threats. I used deceit to do these things, but there was no malice in my mind! If you threaten my people with that same cruelty, and I am forced to conquer you, why should I not have your power as I have theirs?"*

"Because Man, for all the beauty of his works, will forever have evil in his heart. I am happy to see your fires, though they remind me of lost Mountain. I am happy to see your mirrors, though they bring to mind lost Sun. But were you to possess my power also, the three combined would be greater than the three separate. That power would corrupt you, SutaKe, and the world would suffer. Put it from your mind."

SutaKe said nothing.

"Now, I have a long, long journey to make." Moon wept another stream of stars. "The longest, I think, that ever will be. Farewell,*

HoluKo. Farewell for eternity." And Moon began to drift up through the stars.

"Wait!" shouted SutaKe, after her back.

Moon paused.

"What I propose is not a challenge. Not like the other two, at least. And I give you my word there is no trick in it. Yours is the power over life and death, and never will I claim it. Only, do not take our loved ones too high for us to see. There may be evil in us, that I cannot deny, but kindness overwhelms it. Please, Moon. The contest I propose will show this, if only you will stay to listen."

Moon descended once again, though still she remained more distant than before. "I will hear the details of your contest," she said, "but I make no further promise."

"I propose a contest of gifts." SutaKe was glad, at least, that Moon was not already gone. "There is no trick here. Each of us will bestow three gifts upon the other. Whoever gives the greatest gifts will be the victor, only, hear me out. It is not the winning of the contest that matters here. You are powerful, Moon, and surely have great gifts to give. But if I can give away still greater wonders, it will show that kindness outshines evil in my heart. Man would not merely have won your presence: he would have proven himself worthy! Think on this, Moon, see that there is no trick, and accept if you are willing."

For hours, the HoluKo waited, watching Moon's face in the sky. And for those hours, Moon thought hard. SutaKe was right, she realised. If his gift was greater than her own, it would show that Man's little evil was no cause for fear. But still Moon was suspicious, and rightly so, for SutaKe's contest did hold a trick, and a very subtle one at that.

SutaKe's craftsmen had made a vast number of mirrors to vanquish Sun, and such great practice had lent them skill in the art the like of which has never since been seen. Moon, he was sure, could grant gifts just as grand, but—crucially—no grander. Goods, he knew, were not the kindest gift. To win the contest, Moon would have to give something more. But the only greater thing she had to give was her enduring presence, and with it the departed spirits who walked her shores. Thus, SutaKe knew that even if he lost the contest, he would win his prize.

Moon's great mind was not as sharp as SutaKe's and she did not realise the trick. Nevertheless, Moon had seen both Sun and Mountain bested in this way, and so was still suspicious. "I agree that this contest is fair," she said. "If you win, you will truly have proven yourself kind. And if I win, I will make my journey as I planned." Truthfully, Moon did not want to live in even greater loneliness, high in the heavens, and so she was happy that SutaKe had made this wager. However, she was wiser than the other elements—too wise to let joy cloud her judgement. "However," she continued, "I have seen your tricks before. If you are not truly kind, if you do not win this contest or seek only to deceive, I give myself the right to deal out a greater punishment for your past misdeeds. Now you think on this arrangement, SutaKe. If your challenge is a trick, withdraw it now. Wrong me, and my wrath will make your present penalty seem kind."

SutaKe did think. He thought very carefully indeed. Though Mountain could sear and Sun scorch, Moon's power was subtler, and far more terrible. But SutaKe was cunning, and felt confident in his great plan. Moon's new wrath could not be so harsh that it destroyed the winning gift, and so at the very least, the HoluKo would have their departed loved ones still. Also, SutaKe was confident in his craftsmen: the mirror-makers and Stonemen were skilled indeed, and it seemed possible even that this contest could be won in earnest. "What you suggest is fair," he said at last. "I wish that you could see that I deceived your companions only because they became a threat to my people. However, I can understand your trepidation. It is reasonable that you should have some assurance that I have no trick in mind."

And so the contest of gifts began. For three days and three nights, the HoluKo women set about weaving a fine cloak for Moon, with soft fibres dyed in solid, substantial colours. The cloak was a garment like none made since. Its weave was so fine that neither water nor air could find its way through the fabric, and its hue was dark and rich as night.

In return, Moon gave to SutaKe a collar woven from the reeds of her own white island. Taken from beyond the In-between, that fabric would never wear and was more beautiful than anything the mortal island could produce. Anything, that was, except Moon's new cloak, which was easily its rival. But the first gift, SutaKe had always known, would be the least lavish and so he had held back the mirror-makers for a later exchange. Moon, clearly, had thought the same. SutaKe put on his woven collar, and has worn it ever since. Moon put on her cloak and turned in admiration. Moon turns still, though very slowly: you can see this in the sky at night.

"It seems that these gifts are evenly matched," said Moon, turning slowly in the sky. "Your gift to me is kind indeed, but no kinder than mine, you must admit."

"I do admit it," said SutaKe. "But my next gift to you shall be grander."

"As shall mine to you."

And so ended the first exchange of gifts. Immediately, SutaKe set his mirror-makers to work on the second. This was a great mirror—far greater than the one he had used to trick Sun into giving out his light—and all of one perfect piece of stone. The Stonemen worked a day and a night to bring it from the quarry, and for two more days and two more nights, the mirror-makers set about polishing its surface to a flawless sheen. So lustrous was that obsidian glass that the light it gave off was twelve times as bright as that it took in—the image ten times clearer than unvarnished sight.

In exchange for this most precious gift, Moon gave a wondrous sword. Once again, its substance had come from the white island itself. The wood that formed its body, no stone could break, and the many pitch-set blades that formed its edge would never shatter. So sharp were these that they could cut not only the matter, but the spirit of a man: for the spirits on the white island use such things themselves. SutaKe took up his sword, and Moon gazed into her mirror.

"In truth," said Moon, "your gift is the more finely crafted." She put the mirror before her face, and from the island all the HoluKo saw Moon's light filtered through the ruddy stone. Moon does not often do this now, but sometimes, if you are lucky, you can see it in the sky at night. "However," Moon continued, "the thing that I have given you is like nothing the island has seen before. I have mirrors here that, while nowhere near as fine, are comparable in form. By this token, I believe *the value of our gifts is equal once again."*

"I will admit," said SutaKe, "that this sword is special. There is no other like it on the island, and though I have not seen the mirrors you possess, I can believe that they may be almost as beautiful as the one I have given you. Though your gift to me is not so fine, its rarity, I think, makes its worth just as great." He admitted this, but was still confident: his greatest gift, he had reserved for last. Moon's third gift must either be a lesser one, costing her the contest, or the greatest gift she could bestow, which was the one the HoluKo wanted. Whether or not he won this wager, SutaKe would be the victor overall. "My next gift shall be grander still."

"As shall mine."

And so ended the second exchange of gifts, and so began the third, for SutaKe set his Stonemen and mirror-makers—and once again the weaving women—to work without delay. This gift, he knew, would require all the skill of all his artisans, and it would have significance beyond its form. Every effort did he make to keep its nature hidden from Moon, since Moon's surprise would enhance the power of this final gift. But Moon could not hide her work like this. For three full days, while women wove, Stonemen knapped and mirror-makers polished, Moon glowed with a peculiar light, and SutaKe knew that her gift this time must be more than mere shaped stone or woven fibre.

At long last—nine days and nights since the contest began, and longer than the quarrels with Sun and Mountain combined—the contest was complete. Moon sat blue in the morning sky, faded from her exertions. SutaKe and his artisans felt much the same fatigue, though they could only sit upon the dusty ground about the fire. But at long last, SutaKe knew, he had won his wager.

"Moon," called SutaKe. "Though thus far our gifts are matched, equal in weight of utility and form, I think this one can tip the scales. Behold." And he held up a grand glass mask, of the sort that warriors wear in honoured battle. Its shape was the perfect likeness of a human face, carved to perfection by all the Stonemen. Its surface was the clear equal of Moon's mirror, mimicking the world with the same sharpness, the same light, its sheen ground in by all the mirror-makers. And the straps that would hold it to the face were of a fine and cunning weave,

*devised by all the women of the tribe. Not before the quarrel with Sun,
SutaKe knew, had there ever been such artisans as graced the HoluKo
with their presence now. And so he knew without a doubt that not
even the spirits on the white island could boast such skill in crafts.*

*Moon had few words. "Truly no item I can give could show such
excellence as this."*

*"Thank you, Moon. I made this mask so that, even if your gift
was greater, even if you drifted high into the heavens as you intend, you
would still have at least our likeness to keep you company. I hope that
this is well-received."*

*Moon smiled, but she shed stars also, so the HoluKo could see not
all was well. "SutaKe, this is well-received indeed. So thoughtful is
your gift that I am pained to say that you have lost this contest. No
item I can give could match this mask, but what I give is greater than
any item."*

"What your gift?" All the tribe wanted to know.

*"It is life, SutaKe. Eternal life. Can your mask match this? Can
it prevent my light from fading? Can it preserve my strength for all the
years?"*

*Suddenly, SutaKe saw how this wager had been won. Mountain
and Sun had been strong indeed, but Moon possessed a cunning that
could rival his own. "No," he whispered.*

*"Though I could see no trick in this contest when we began, the
lavishness of your gifts let me see that no goods I had to give could win
in this exchange. It was inevitable that now, at the end, I would have
to yield at least a little of my power. I began to see how, even should I
win, this contest of gifts would always serve you in the end. But I am
not without cunning, SutaKe. My gift has won, and yet I still possess
the right to soar away. Is this not so?"*

"It is."

*"And do you remember what was agreed? As your contest was a
trick like the two before—and I have won besides—I am now entitled
to deal out a wrath even greater than my absence."*

*"I remember. But this agreement was between us alone: whatever
wrath you hold, give it to me, and do not punish the HoluKo for the
deeds I alone have done."*

"It is already done. My gift is your new punishment, SutaKe. I will rise high in the heavens, as I had planned: high above the reach of the HoluKo, but higher still above your own. I have made it so you cannot die, and so not even in death will you see those who have been lost. For all eternity, you will walk the island alone: alone even among your tribe."

The full gravity of the Moon's curse now dawned on SutaKe. "Is there no other way?"

"No. There will be no more wagers. High in the heavens, I shall not hear them. And even if I did, there is nothing I could do. This gift has greatly weakened me. I cannot take it back any more than I could give it for a second time."

"Then this final ploy has brought me only pain."

"Not only." Moon smiled. "Your gifts were kind indeed: kind enough that I will not rise quite so high as I had planned. Always will my light shine on the island, though looking up, you shall not see the spirits on my shores. And the journey will not be so long that the members of your tribe cannot come to me when their time is upon them. I am right to fear Man. Your contest has proved me right in this, but also it has made me sorry that it must be so. Keep your mask, SutaKe. You forged it for an enemy: I cannot take it as a friend."

And so Moon drifted high into the stars—though not so high that she cannot be seen—and SutaKe put on his face of glass. He wears it still, as a reminder of that challenge, and to hide his shame. But now the island is ruled by Man alone: not Mountain nor Sun nor Moon can challenge his hard-won right. And so in that first and last defeat, there is enduring victory, that even this sad tale can tell.

It was a fine ending—and sitting before Tribe-mother and Tribe-father, SutaKe did not think he had ever heard it told so well—but it was not entirely true. A fourth tale there should have been, telling of SutaKe's fourth and final trick: the trick that conquered Moon's cruel curse. But never would that tale be told. The only person who could tell it— nameless now—had made his spirit-journey to the white island a very, very long time ago.

21
THREE TALES

The KasseKo's reaction to the Moon tale was not as SutaKe had hoped. None voiced approval, and many spoke to one another in hushed and unkind tones. Tribe-father's mouth was one hard line beneath his mask.

Tribe-mother frowned, and raised her eyes in thought. "That was not like the tales of our tribe. Nevertheless, I am glad to have heard it. And are you the same 'SutaKe' as the one who spoke with Moon?"

"Yes."

"This is curious indeed."

"I do not believe it." Tribe-father stood, the obsidian dagger unsheathed once more. He pointed it at SutaKe. "If you are the SutaKe from that tale, then you cannot die. This is easily tested."

"Of course. But it would be most dishonourable to harm a visitor in such a way. Especially a visitor who has yet to give you his message."

"Then give your message."

"No."

"No?" Tribe-father took a step forward, brandishing the knife. "You dare..."

Again came Tribe-mother's hand, placed gently upon his arm. "This was supposed to be an exchange of gifts, my dear: we still have our tale to tell. But that is easily remedied." She looked up at SutaKe. "And then we will be done humouring this foreign chief."

"Very well," Tribe-father growled. "Then hurry up and let's be done with it."

Tribe-mother stretched her back and settled down ready to tell her tale.

In ancient days when the island was new, a crab that scuttled about the beach began to grow unhappy. When it walked beneath the water, it was cold and wet. When it walked upon the sand, it was hot and dry.

"If only I could scuttle up amongst the clouds," the crab wished aloud. "The clouds look comfortably cool and moist. If I were to scuttle up there, surely I would be comfortable, and surely I could be happy."

But the crab had not wished only to itself. It was surprised to see a gull flap down before it, and so—as crabs do—buried itself beneath the sand, leaving only its stalky eyes poking up.

"Do not be afraid!" The gull looked all around, swivelling its head because it could no longer see the crab. "Though normally we would be foes, your suffering has moved me. Climb upon my back, little crab, and I will take you to the soaring clouds."

The crab was most suspicious—it is true that crab and gull have always been at odds—but, after a great deal of coaxing, did as the gull had asked. The crab was pleased to find that the gull had spoken true: it stood very still, keeping its deadly beak tucked tightly against its breast.

"Thank you, gull," said the crab, clinging onto its feathers with tiny nippers. "This is kind of you indeed."

And indeed it was, for the gull had truly been moved by the crab's words, and had no malice whatsoever in its heart. Exactly as it had offered, it took the crab up to the clouds.

But the crab was not at all pleased with what it found there.

"Why," said the crab, *"this is worse than sea or sand! Water positively pours from this land of heaven, and the sun lies far too close above! What an awful place this is!*

The gull was...

Suddenly, SanaRo spoke. "The gull was offended, because the sky was its home. It said to the crab: 'Clearly you will not be happy anywhere! Sitting moping in sea, sand and sky, there is only one way you could ever bring happiness to the world.' And so the gull smashed the crab against a wide, flat rock and ate the soft flesh inside. And this is why, even when one is not content with what they bring, one must not be ungrateful for the kind deeds of others."

The KasseKo stared. Some reached for clubs or spears, so rude had SanaRo been. But Tribe-mother calmed them with a wave of her hand. "That is an old tale indeed, but it was the first that sprang to mind and I thought our guests might yet enjoy it. No matter. I have many, many more. Let's see..."

SutaKe looked around while Tribe-mother thought. Many of the KasseKo glared, but still more had forgiven the interruption, dismissing SanaRo's bad conduct as nothing more than some foreign quirk.

Once again, Tribe-mother settled herself down to tell a tale.

In ancient days when the island was new, a boar and a beetle walked together through the forest.

"Careful, friend!" cried the beetle. "I am afraid that you might step on me!"

"And well you should be," said the boar, "for I am big and you are small. It is proper that the weak should be cautious of the strong, but the strong have no reason to be cautious of the weak."

"Ah," said the beetle. "That is all well and good for the strongest to say, but you or I would be better off if only we could all agree to care for one another."

"What was that? 'You or I?' Why, I have no reason to prefer

such an arrangement: who on the island could be stronger than the boar?"

"I admit that I can think of no one right away, but still I do not believe you are the strongest creature here."

"Bah! Nobody is stronger than I am. What could be more powerful than my fine tusks? What could be more sturdy than my solid trotters?"

"Perhaps you are right." The beetle paused for a moment. "But your strength is not without bounds. Surely you must agree that this is so?"

"I agree with no such thing! I could perform any feat of strength that you demand."

"Very well," said the...

SanaRo spoke once again. "The beetle demanded that the boar uproot the greatest tree on the island, taller than all its brothers and seated in the hardest earth. Without hesitation, the boar went to work. Its tusks easily tore up even that hard ground, and one strong charge with lowered head sent the tree toppling. But the instant that its branches touched the ground, a great swarm of bees rose up and threw themselves against the boar, leaving stinging welts all over its face.

"'Why, boar!' said the beetle. 'Didn't you know about the nest in that great tree?'

"'Oooh.' Boar scraped his face against the rocks, trying to rid himself of the stings. 'No, I didn't know about the nest! Why didn't you tell me that the bees were there?'

"'I didn't think it mattered. Why would a big strong boar like you need to concern himself with a little nest of weak bees?'

"And this is why we should always be wary of whom we might offend, lest our carelessness comes to harm us in the end."

The KasseKo had waited while SanaRo finished the tale, but clearly they were not amused.

Tribe-father spoke through gritted teeth, his two-skull

mask clacking with the tremblings of his rage. "This Storyteller would do well to learn from his own parable."

But again came Tribe-mother's hand to calm him. "What you say is true. It does not do to interrupt a tale. But there are more that I can tell, and save this message-bringing ceremony. Come." She turned to a woman sitting close by. "Bring me some water, while I recall another tale to tell."

SutaKe looked around while Tribe-mother sipped. All the KasseKo had now taken up arms, and though they still sat frozen, waiting about the fire, it seemed that it was not the story they were waiting for. He had known that they would not stand his game for long, and it seemed that this round would have to be the last. He watched Tribe-mother regard the empty gourd bowl, having finished her drink, and thought that he could guess the next tale to be told. In their violent isolation, the KasseKo had accumulated all manner of brilliant ornaments and fine arms, but almost never could they trade tales with other tribes.

Tribe-mother began.

In ancient days when the island was new, a foolish boy snuck inside a warlock's cave. Intending to steal a sweet snack of honey, he opened up a gourd...

"The gourd has an evil spirit inside. The spirit says 'Now that you have freed me from the gourd, I will do my evil and sink the world!' but the boy says that he doesn't believe that such a great spirit could have fitted into such a small gourd. The spirit gets back in to prove it can, and the boy seals it up once more. This is the oldest tale of all."

A roar went up around the KasseKo. Tribe-father snatched up his knife and leapt forward, wide eyes staring through the mask. "Either keep your servant silent, or I will silence him myself!" This time, Tribe-mother did nothing to calm him.

"No," said SutaKe.

"No?" Tribe-father took another step forward, shifting

the hilt of the blade in his grasp.

"No." SutaKe spread his arms wide. "He is right to do it."

The KasseKo were silent. Tribe-father's anger seemed almost to have boiled over. He said nothing, and instead simply stood there, shaking.

SutaKe explained. "We told you our tale. It was a good tale—a very good tale indeed—and one that I believe has never before left our tribe. Yet you tell us only old fables that everyone has heard. Our stories were to be gifts to one another, but you have offered a poor exchange indeed. Had we given you a fine new bow, would you have repaid us with a crooked old arrow?"

The whole tribe was standing now, tense and ready. They hissed like snakes, shaking clubs and rattling bones. It was like the sound that they had made while chasing the boar.

SutaKe ignored them. Out of habit, he arched his eyebrows, though they were invisible beneath the mask. He stared at Tribe-father. "No?"

Tribe-father continued to stand and grind his teeth.

"Then do not try to swindle us with tales worn beyond repair."

"This is like the exchange in your story," said Tribe-mother, calmly. "Like the sword, that was new, against the mirror, which was like things seen before. The novelty of your tale gives it worth greater than ours."

"That is true."

"Then you have left us with a debt that we cannot repay!" Tribe-father spoke once more. "This is like the warlock's magic! Never could we do such magic, and so never could we pay him back in kind! This is the warlock's trick once more!"

The KasseKo tightened their circle around SutaKe and SanaRo. Warriors hefted clubs, each one eager to be the first to strike a blow. For just a moment, it seemed as though all had gone horribly wrong.

Then, Tribe-father spoke again. "Long did RanaZo hold this tribe in servitude. Many were the hours given to him. Great was the tribute offered. But still I miss him dearly." He chuckled. "I would pay ten times that price to restore him to the world."

Still the tribe held their weapons ready.

"Put away your spears!" Smiling below his two-skull mask, Tribe-father addressed the circle before speaking to SutaKe. "I thought it strange that you should come here with no thought for your own security. This is an old trick done a new way, and for tradition's sake I honour it. Tell us your message, and know that we will owe a favour to you."

22
AN OMEN

The atmosphere of danger about the camp of the KasseKo had utterly evaporated. Now that they were no immediate threat, SutaKe considered, they were not so different from the other tribes. And the spirit had been right: locked firmly in their timeless ways, they would not be swayed as the DanaKo had. "Do you know of the Steelmen who have come to the island?"

"They trespassed on our land a long time ago." Tribe-father gestured to a trio of helmets by one of the tents. Wooden horns had been bound skilfully to the sides of these steel trophies, possibly to drive away their vengeful spirits. "We have not encountered them much since. RanaZo took great interest in their works, and once bade my warriors study their camp closer, but never did he ask us to carry a message. He, like us, cared more for the heart of the island than for its shores."

"Then I think you will need to hear what I have to say. Oltak, the leader of the Steelmen, has offered trades to all the tribes but yours. And of those, all but the HoluKo accepted what he offered."

"This is what you came to tell us?" Tribe-mother was surprised. "You should know that we do not care much for the swapping of trinkets."

"Oltak does not offer mere trinkets. He brought weapons—forged in his exotic land—like nothing any Stoneman can create, and yet he brought them in great quantity. You have seen these things, I think." He took out the little steel knife to show.

"We took some from the warriors who trespassed here, but they are blunt now." Tribe-father leaned forward, speaking quietly. "No skill nor magic I possess can restore their sharpness."

SutaKe nodded. "This is Oltak's doing: he played a trick like mine. At first the trades he made were generous, and the proudest chieftains rushed to take them. But once those chieftains were loyal to him—once the power of steel had corrupted them—he began to use them. With their force to use as threat, he began to offer worse trades to smaller tribes, who accepted only out of fear. By the time word reached us, he had grown so strong on stolen power that even the DanaKo—with whom I know you have warred in the past—dared not refuse the trade he offered."

"Now I see why you brought this news," said Tribe-father. "You were right—if also bold—to seek our help. Neither the Steelmen nor any of the coastal tribes can take the mountain from us."

"That may be true, but it is not enough. With the tricks of his wealth, Oltak has formed a fearsome army, made of many tribes and armed with steel. Against such numbers and such strength, nothing—not your magic, not your land, not the skill of your warriors—can twist victory from their grasp. If that army marches on the mountain, both our tribes will fall."

The KasseKo began to murmur. Tribe-father spoke: "But if you have come here, you must see a way to solve this problem. Why is it that you need the KasseKo?"

"Though Oltak's army is vast, it will also be slow, and presently it is divided. Were we to defend the mountain, or even retreat all the way to the island's northern shores, they would eventually march and destroy us. However, if we attack Oltak's stronghold—swiftly, and without provocation—then he will have only the support of his nearest tribes. It would take more than a day for him to send a message to the farthest others, and longer still for them to reach the field of battle."

"And this will give us our advantage?"

"I think 'advantage' is too strong a word. It would give us a chance where otherwise there would be none, but Oltak has no doubt surrounded himself with his strongest supporters. Those loyal to him will be well-armed indeed, and will fight as strongly to protect this villain as they would the noblest chief. The DanaKo are trying to sway their neighbours to join our cause, but even if they succeed in every case this battle will be of a scale never seen before. Its outcome will affect us all, and that is why I came to you: beyond tricks and tales, every one of us has a part to play. It is only right that you know yours, even if our tribes have never before been friends."

"Then we are glad that you have come," said Tribe-mother. "But you should know our tribes are not friends even now. However great the coming battle, it still decides only the affairs of Man, and we KasseKo guard the mountain with a greater cause in mind. But for the time being our fates are intertwined, and this alliance shall be the favour to repay your tale." She turned once again to her attendant. "Have the hunters bring meat to the fire, and open up new stores of fruit and nuts. This is a rare occasion: we should mark it with a feast."

In this custom, too, the KasseKo proved to be not unlike the other tribes. But still they were different in the way that they observed it. Rather than melodious songs, there was only the same sibilant chanting that SutaKe had heard in the forest, though he thought the ancient words may well have changed. The instruments, too, were not the same as those used by the HoluKo or the DanaKo. Where usually there would be a crowd of tuned drums, here there were only the bone rattles he had heard from the hunt. Seeing this, SutaKe was most surprised to hear a melody. Looking about, he saw that it was played by just one man, with just one instrument: a line of wooden blocks carefully laid out upon a stand. When struck, each one produced a different sound, and so this musician could do the work of many drummers. The tune he played was lively, and lent a joyful sound to that once sinister chant, though beneath this there could still be heard the sound of finger bones on strings.

The feast itself was rich and good. Without such stocks of tubers as the other tribes, the KasseKo ate a great quantity of meat from the forest, and all manner of strange things that grew upon its trees. They also took the time to gather grubs and insects that few other people would bother to seek out. Not all of these were pleasant, however, and SutaKe suspected that no tribe with ripe crops in their fields would think to try them. Alongside the sweet fruits and berries were bitter roots, though some of the KasseKo chewed on these with great relish, tearing the fibres with practiced teeth.

When the feast was over, SutaKe lay down to sleep. He had grown used to the spirit's presence now, and expected to slip effortlessly into the In-between to meet it. It had orchestrated the tribe's entire campaign, and having heard its tale of new usurping gods, he felt sure that its concerns truly were his own. But despite having found a new ally in the KasseKo—a victory that would surely bring new power to the spirit—he found his dream-journey difficult. When finally he found the spirit, seated before RanaZo's cave, it held its faceless head in its hands and would not speak. Its flesh seemed wooden, rooted to the ground, and all about it tiny boars and scuttling beetles—each one grotesquely disproportioned—tried to break it from the rock below.

"I have done the thing you asked." SutaKe removed his mask.

The spirit looked no stronger. It still sat hunched, head in hands, the creatures crawling all across it. It said nothing.

"The KasseKo will fight with us. I have done what you said to do." He stepped forward.

Still the spirit would not speak.

SutaKe looked all about, searching for some kind of sign, and was surprised to hear the rich clang of steel on stone. The spirit had not moved, but in the stone before it there was a footprint—a footprint with no toes—and resting in this was the blade of steel, just as he had shown it to Tribe-father. If there was meaning in this gesture, SutaKe could not see it.

"Please," he said. "You must tell me what to do. I cannot lead this battle without you! And I fear, even with the KasseKo, our army is not strong."

There was a noise like insects buzzing, but it was quiet.

"What are you saying?"

The noise became louder, but still was faint. SutaKe waited, but it would not grow.

"I cannot hear you."

The noise grew louder still: loud enough for SutaKe to realise there was no sense in it. The spirit's hands muffled what it spoke. Reaching out, he gently pulled them from its face.

Two words drifted from the void: "Look away."

Suddenly, the buzzing became a roar. Where before only the spirit's eyes had burned, its entire face was an inferno, and it spread. The flames poured down the spirit's shoulders and trickled down its chest, setting all the wood ablaze. Tiny creatures scattered, squealing, away from the heat, and SutaKe too. He was only faintly aware of movement as the spirit leant forwards, stretching out a hand.

Then, as quickly as it had started, it was done. SutaKe looked back to where the spirit had been, but could see only a small pile of white ash on a patch of scorched rock. But it was not only that. The knife had melted in the footprint, flooding it with a perfect layer of molten steel.

"What does this mean?" SutaKe called to the glowing air.

But the spirit was gone now, and the dream gave no reply.

23

THE POWER OF STONE

In preparation for the coming battle, both the HoluKo
and the DanaKo joined the KasseKo at an old village
site on a ridge south of the mountain. Just as the spirit
had warned—and HanaRa had feared—GabuKe had not
had great success with his attempts to win over the
chieftains of the nearby tribes. Those who had chosen to
stand against Oltak had been swayed mostly by the
knowledge that the KasseKo would fight for the same
cause. However, this news had driven just as many
chieftains away. SutaKe had little doubt that at least some
of these would try to warn their new tyrant, in order to gain
his favour. For that reason, there was no preparation, no
hesitation. Neither did SutaKe make any attempt to speak
with the spirit.

The spirit was not dead. It certainly was not without
power. But nevertheless, it was gone. Without the fires of
its eyes, SutaKe's dreams were cold and empty in a way that
they had never been since he had left RanaZo's cave. With
that last, sudden fire, the spirit had robbed the In-between

of all its light. Without its guidance, SutaKe thought, the fate of the island looked just as dim.

But there was someone else. Someone SutaKe had trusted for far longer. He found HanaRa mending arrows in the last low light of the day. Tomorrow, the warriors would set off for Oltak's stronghold, and the final battle would begin.

"Should you not be with the other chieftains?" HanaRa smiled. "I'm sure there is still much to be done."

"Nothing that will make much difference now." SutaKe lowered himself clumsily to the ground and adjusted the stony weight of his mask. "I have spent too much time with chieftains of late."

HanaRa laughed. "Given what you're trying to do, that hardly seems like it should be unexpected."

"Actually, there are...two things I have been trying to do." SutaKe hoped HanaRa would remember their last conversation, though it seemed so long ago. "One thing that must be done for the benefit of the whole island, and that will be decided tomorrow, for better or worse. And...one other thing. A much smaller thing, but one that was a promise. I fear that thing may never be done."

HanaRa set down her pitch and feathers. "Now is not the time to worry about that." Her face was stern, but she looked tired, too. But then, after the journey around the mountain, everyone looked tired. "There will be plenty of time when the battle is done."

"But when the battle is done, things will go back to the way they were before."

"Isn't that what you wanted?"

"Only for the tribe."

"Well then. That is what a good chief does."

"What if..." SutaKe wondered how much he could say. "What if I am not a good chief?"

HanaRa said nothing. She only stared.

"What if my bringing the tribes to battle was not my

work at all?"

"It was." HanaRa spoke firmly. "GabuKe has helped. Tribe-mother and Tribe-father too. And the other small tribes will assist you on the field of battle. But it was you who brought them here. Without your work, none of this could have been done. Yes, others have helped, but you have more than earned their aid."

SutaKe thought of the spirit. Had he not summoned it? Had he not brought RanaZo the potion? But no. The spirit had its grudge against the gods who overthrew it. It had its pity for the HoluKo, who without its power would share its fate. He had not earned the spirit's help. Perhaps that was why it had left him now. "You're right, HanaRa. Thank you." He loathed the obsidian mask for the burdens it had brought, but at that particular moment he was glad to have it. He could not have lied to her otherwise.

The following day's journey was not a long one. Oltak's stronghold stood in a great expanse of flat land, halfway between the mountain ridge and the shore, and it was truly extraordinary. A vast tower of wooden planks stretched up, peering over a tall wood fence, and around this had been built up a further obstacle: a ditch, a high bank of fresh-packed soil, and countless sharpened stakes all jutting out. Oltak had not merely secured the allegiance of the local tribes: he had sculpted the very land to serve his will. GabuKe had told of this thing before, but without seeing its scale, its might, it was hard to appreciate the power it could command. Here on the flat, this fortress seemed to cast a shadow greater even than the mountain itself.

In the shadow of the fortress, smaller buildings stood. These were made of poles and bound reeds: the dwellings of the puppet-chiefs and all their tribesmen. Even out of direct light, the gleam of steel was all around. GabuKe had sought over all the island for soldiers willing to fight, SutaKe had struggled hard to win the warriors of the KasseKo, but Oltak's army was just as large, and during

SutaKe's hard toil, they had waited in the shade.

Seeing the force marching down from the mountain, these warriors put on new armour and took up their arms. They seemed to be in no great hurry. Looking out along the coast, now he was clear of the forest's trees, SutaKe could see smoke rising far away along the beach. There was another tribe not yet even present, and not far away. A runner darted out from the huts around the fortress, hurrying towards the village smoke. If Oltak did not already have the advantage, he would soon.

Almost instinctively, SutaKe's army put on new speed. Not a run yet, but not far off. The bone rattles of the KasseKo began to shake once again. It was a steady, regular rhythm to match the pace of the warriors' feet. As the fortress loomed and the charge began, it was joined by the familiar hunters' chant. Hearing this, Oltak's army seemed to show some fear, but still they did not falter. Forming into one solid line—shields overlapping as they had done in the hands of the Steelmen—the conquered tribes prepared to fight. Though not as familiar with the new exotic weapons as they had been with their own, SutaKe could see their ranks were as strong as those of the foreign warriors at the ruins. There would be no pillar this time. Nor could the HoluKo simply hold the high ground against assault. This battle would decide the fate of the island, and it would be fought on the flat.

Arrows lashed down from the tower like the first drops of rain before a storm. Several warriors fell, but SutaKe took pride in seeing how few of the fort's windows had been manned. Oltak had few archers of his own now, and those among the puppet-tribes—fighting among the warriors, as always—had none of the advantage of the tower's height. Some tried to make use of the raised earth bank, but these soon found themselves easy targets for the opposing archers, protected by SutaKe's tribe. Soon, sword and spear and shield took over where bow could do no more. The lines of warriors met with a crash of metal, wood and stone, and the rhythmic chanting of the KasseKo at last gave way to the chaotic din of war.

The steel-ringed shields offered great protection to the defending line, but standing in such close formation they were quickly surrounded by the charging mass. SutaKe himself struck what might have been the first blow, parrying the stab of a steel spear before lunging forward with the stone head of his own. BaraKa, next to him in the battle-line, tried to force his way in where that warrior had fallen, but two more had already closed the gap. This happened all along the shield-wall. Wherever a warrior fell, those around him shifted to fill the place. But though this defence would not allow any attacker to pass through the line, the mass itself was forced to give up ground. Against the force of the HoluKo and DanaKo, the army might have resisted. Against the KasseKo, however, no strength could be enough, for it was fear they fought then, and fear that pushed them back.

Here, the fortifications of Oltak's stolen land proved to be his greatest mistake. Suddenly, without SutaKe even having seen the threat behind, the warrior he opposed toppled back, tumbling down the steep earth ditch and onto the stakes below. It was only this grisly warning, and a swift hand from BaraKa, that stopped the chieftain of the HoluKo from sharing his grim fate.

Many others of the puppet-tribes fell in this same way. Still more were forced to risk a scramble through the stakes, and though this was far less dangerous than an unguided fall, the spears that waited when they turned their backs proved just as deadly. For the few who crossed unscathed—following in the footsteps of their tribes' archers, still waiting beyond the barrier—no hope waited but surrender. It was quickly made, but still the arrows came whipping down from Oltak's tower. Then, suddenly, there was a shouted order in some foreign tongue, and the onslaught ceased.

A face appeared at one of the windows, and SutaKe recognised it as the interpreter who had spoken in the Great Hut, before the DanaKo came. "Oltak of the Red Turtle is disgusted by this senseless violence," he called down. "He is loath to make deals with such savages as you, but to prevent further bloodshed he is prepared to offer terms like before."

"Your master is in no position to make such an offer!" GabuKe shouted. "His fortress may be proof against our spears, but any wood can be consumed by flame."

"Send a messenger out towards the beach. My master thinks that, if you could see what he can see, you would not hesitate to accept."

On his own initiative, SanaRo dashed out to the place where the land dropped away towards the sea. He was not long in returning. "There is another army approaching," he panted. "It is more than one tribe. This..." he paused for breath again. "This was not half of the Steelman's force."

SutaKe looked to SanaRo. He had not seen the army on the beach, but in the Stoneman's face he could see there was no hope.

"My master is impatient for your answer."

SutaKe hesitated, waiting desperately for the spirit, somehow, to intervene. But it was not to be. "I..." He was interrupted.

"Then we will not make him wait!" An arrow howled up over the wall, striking the interpreter square in the face. He toppled out of sight.

SutaKe could not find HanaRa when he looked around, but there could be no doubt that it had been her voice. She was not permitted here on the field of battle any more than she had been in the Great Hut, but for better or for worse, she had decided the result of this last meeting just as she had swayed the outcome of the first. But the army made no move to respond to the approaching horde. If there was a victory to be had here, it would be for honour alone.

But then SutaKe could hear the buzzing of flies once again. Quiet at first, but then as loud as it had been in his dreams, and louder still, until it was a roar that everyone could hear. But the voice, SutaKe knew, was for him alone. "Look away," the spirit said. "Look away."

There was fire on the mountain. Smoke, black and opaque as full-burned wood, blotted out the sun, and the entire southern half of the island was plunged into a midday night. SutaKe called for the army to retreat, but there was no need. All were already running for the relative safety of the nearby ridge, raised high enough from the flat to offer some protection from the mountain's wrath. In the tower, the Steelmen hurried back and forth, not sure whether it was best to throw open the gates and flee, or to stay and test their shelter against the ash. Reaching the crest of the ridge at last, SutaKe chose to disregard the spirit's words. He looked back, and saw from there the army on the beach.

There was a sudden blast from the mountaintop, and something rolled quickly down the slope. SutaKe had been wrong: a pillar would decide this battle. But instead of stone, this was a pillar of boiling ash. It passed through the forest in a flash, tearing up as many trees as it consumed and leaving the land behind it in a burning haze of grey. The armoured soldiers, as before, tried to throw themselves from the pillar's path, but it was useless now. The ash poured across a stretch of beach two miles wide, throwing up huge clouds of steam as the waves met, resisted, and failed to stop its blazing assault. With a noise like thunder, the pillar of ash rolled on across the sea. Its haze prevented SutaKe from seeing the aftermath of its onslaught on the beach, but there would be, he knew, nothing left to see.

And still the mountain's work was not yet done. Tendrils of liquid flame trickled down its shoulders, glowing brightly in its self-made night. With all the deliberation of a much smaller creature, the searing wind changed direction, and the stronghold was almost blotted out of sight. The few Steelmen who had fled the fort were almost clear. Tongues of flame upon its walls showed little hope for those still inside. Yet there was one figure—no, two—neither within the fortress nor on the ridge. On that slope below the ruins, SutaKe had been forced to acknowledge the Steelmen's bravery, but on this slope was one who demanded his respect. Heaving an injured comrade along beside him, he stumbled on through the burning haze. Despite the protestations of the HoluKo—HanaRa's the loudest voice amongst them—SutaKe hurried down to help the warrior.

Below the ridge, the air was choking. Occasional wafts—whether swayed by the wind or sent directly from the mountain—rendered it from time to time too hot to breathe. Glowing embers stung SutaKe's ears, but his mask kept them from his face, and the sweat-soaked collar gave protection too. Head down, skin plastered with ash, the Steelman accepted his help wordlessly, and together they heaved the wounded man to safety. Halfway up the ridge, BaraKa ventured down to carry him, and SutaKe led that brave warrior, eyes squeezed shut against the ash.

Atop the ridge, those Steelmen who had escaped were ringed around by spears. The KasseKo especially were keen to keep them held. But SutaKe sensed that this one who had stopped to help the wounded man could be trusted—perhaps should be rewarded. It was only then, beyond the reach of blazing ash, that he saw the rings on this man's fingers, and the gold stuck in his ears. The strange garments were burned and powdered grey, but there was no doubt that he had rescued Oltak from the hot breath of the mountain. The merchant said nothing. The injured man, SutaKe saw, had an arrow jutting out beside his nose. His face was hidden behind a cake of ash that had formed upon the blood, but there was no doubt that it was the interpreter.

The stronghold could not be seen, but there was a

yellow glow down on the flat where it had been, like a sun under the burnt-black sky. Out to sea, there was a smaller flicker, like the moon to Oltak's sun: in the fierce heat of the rolling ash, the Red Turtle was burning. The spirit had guided SutaKe in all his battles. Finally, conclusively, and with its own power, it had won their war.

"I you bring. Trade."

SutaKe was amazed to hear Oltak speak. The words were slow, and difficult to understand, but they were spoken with the confidence of a leader.

"I you bring, big world." He swept an arm out over the boiling sea, the light of the Red Turtle flickering through the ash and steam. "Now nothing. You nothing. I nothing." Still staring at SutaKe's mask he jabbed a finger at the spark on the waves, emphasising each word: "You. Lose. World!"

This man had been the force behind everything that had happened. Without him, there would have been no war, no mask, no spirit. And yet, confronting him, he seemed so small. He was no more a tyrant now than SutaKe was immortal. Slowly, methodically, he removed all his rings but one and dropped them at the chieftain's feet before striding off to join the soldiers. That last ring, SutaKe later found, had been like a gourd. There was a hollow space inside, holding just enough poison to kill one man.

24
THE WARLOCK'S CAVE

It was two days before the ash stopped pouring from the mountain, and three before the earth beneath was cool. When SutaKe returned to that high ridge, he could barely see where the stronghold had once stood. Oltak's footprint on the land had been erased, just like the footprint in SutaKe's dream. And from closer than the In-between, the spirit spoke.

"Thanks to you, SutaKe, the island is free once more. No more shall new steel threaten the ways of ancient stone. No more shall the tower of the tyrant cast its shadow across the land."

"And that is good," said SutaKe. "But will it last? Oltak came from a vast and wealthy country. There will be others, surely, who come to follow in his footsteps."

"There are no footsteps to follow: the ashes of his stronghold have been scattered to the sea, and that great boat can bring no news back to his land. And should others come of their own accord, the Steelman's plot would never work again. For not only is the island free, it is united. The tribes that follow you have made me strong, and seeing my strength still more have come to follow. Never again can they be set against each other as they were before." The spirit sighed. "As much joy as your success brings, it reminds me also of sad things. When others came to wrest the island from my hand, it did not end so well as this."

The spirit spoke softly now. Whatever trick of its ethereal form had caused its voice to buzz, it had since passed. Even if its status could never truly be restored, SutaKe was glad to have freed it from the prison of the In-between.

"You are right. Whatever happens from now on, I will always remember how fortunate I am, and how much greater the cost could have been."

"Yet still you are not happy."

"I..." Among the tribe, SutaKe was always forced to maintain the old charade. There was no reason why he should not be obliged to do so for the spirit, too. But he had long ago decided that it could not be deceived. "No. You know there is something else that I must do. But I have thought about it for a long, long time—even when the Steelman was foremost in my mind—and I fear now that it can never be done. With this victory over steel, our honoured traditions are as strong as stone, and these are what bring sorrow to me now."

"With my wisdom," said the spirit, "you have done many things you thought could not be done."

"That is true. I have won against an army far vaster than my own, and another armed with better spears. I have secured the allegiance of the friendless KasseKo, and seen the island itself turn against my foes. But these were violent, material things. What can even spirits do to sway the battle between stubborn tradition and unyielding heart?"

The spirit laughed, and SutaKe could hear the wings again. But they were not the wings of insects this time: rather, the wings of birds. "I will show you, but only if you go to where RanaZo now rests his head." The wings fluttered, and it was gone. SutaKe almost felt a breeze as something darted off towards the mountain, and the cave on its far side.

There was to be a feast in the village of the KasseKo. It was not the most inviting of places but, being in the centre of the island, it was the most fair to those small tribes who had travelled the farthest. Besides this, having won against Oltak's forces—and in so spectacular a manner—SutaKe had secured the respect of every tribe, and in his presence none would risk the dishonour that a quarrel would surely bring. This feast gave SutaKe every reason to visit RanaZo's cave once more, but the many feet made the journey slower than he would have liked. Never had the spirit failed to tip the balance of his great battles. Was it possible that it could also intervene in the small matters within his tribe?

Reaching the north face of the mountain, SutaKe could not stand to wait while the feast took place. Drawing away from the vast group of the united tribes, he set off for that winding pumice path that rose up near the marsh.

"Where are you going, SutaKe?" called KanaKa. "Why are you leaving now, without a retinue?"

SutaKe spread wide his arms. "There are no foes left to fear. And having faced so many trials alone, why should I need to be guarded in times of peace?" He tried to dismiss the question, but still it was clear that KanaKa was suspicious. Everyone was. Without revealing the spirit's presence—which, surely, nobody would believe—there was no good reason he could give for leaving then. But, fortunately, his status as chief above the tribes served instead of reason, and nobody trailed after him as he began to skirt around the mountain's foot.

It was peculiar, he considered, how familiar the path up to RanaZo's cave had become. This was the first time he had visited without the threat of wandering KasseKo hunters, and yet he recognised all the little landmarks along the path. Stones with strange shapes. Little trees that pushed up thinly from the rock. Places where, he was sure, the KasseKo had come with hammers and chipped steps into big stones. He remembered these things more clearly even than he did the landmarks of the forest where he had once carried arrows for KanaKa, while the warrior hunted boar. RanaZo's cave was not a home to him by any means, but it was, in its own way, welcoming. It was like the hut of a distant friend: separate, far away, but a welcome shelter nonetheless. Ducking yet again past the chains of shrivelled heads, he stood in the centre, allowing his eyes to adjust to the gloom.

The place was just as he had left it. RanaZo's skull still rested on the stone table, pointed teeth smiling blankly. The heads at the entrance still looked from side to side, stirred by the wind. The bowls and dishes still waited in their orderly chaos, never to be taken up again. Even the conch was the same, still slightly askew from when SanaRo had set it down, his eyes distracted by the KasseKo standing at the door. SutaKe saw that these things were the same, so why had the spirit sent him here?

It spoke suddenly, but SutaKe had long since grown accustomed to its voice. "Did you never wonder why only you could hear me? Why, of all the people on this island, you were the one who I should guide?"

"I did."

"Then you were mistaken. It was not only you with whom I spoke. Have you forgotten the warlock?"

"I had, but he is dead now. What difference does it make?"

"You should know, SutaKe. You freed me from this place, but had RanaZo made his way down from the mountain, he would have walked alone. Before your victory against the DanaKo, I had not faith enough to leave."

As the spirit spoke, the source of its voice drifted farther and farther into the cave. It drifted so far, in fact, that

SutaKe was sure that it had passed beyond the wall of rock at the very back. A wall, SutaKe realised, that was not part of the mountain.

"As spirit I was freed from the warlock's cave, and as spirit alone I have won your material war. But in the war of heart against tradition, no mere spirit can hold sway. Free my body, SutaKe." The chieftain placed his ear against the wall, and the next words echoed through the rock itself. "Bring me back into the world."

25
SUTAKE RETURNS

SutaKe hurried back down the mountain path so quickly that when he reached the village of the KasseKo, the feast had not yet quite begun. He wanted to tell the tribes then. To bring men with hammers and wooden mauls and break down the cave's false wall. But as well as being a mere celebration, the feast would dictate the course of many things to come. SutaKe was well aware of how easily new Steelmen could make the journey to the island, and how easily this war could be repeated. It was essential that, if that were to happen, the tribes could stand together and resist as one. There was also the matter of the captured soldiers. Many tribes had gained great stock of Oltak's foreign weapons, and these soldiers, trained in their use and care, would be invaluable in the years to come. Despite the resentment felt among the island's leaders, not even Tribe-father wished to see them put to death.

GabuKe, whose crown and station were well known by the many tribes, began his speech. "Honoured tribes. The battle that has just been fought was like none the world has ever seen. Seeing what the Steelman brought, who could not have been tempted to serve this tyrant? But when the very island deigns to intervene, who can refuse to take its side? Those who served the Steelman before now stand amongst us, and they stand not as recent foes, but as new friends."

A murmur rose around the great village fire, and it was not entirely content. "We have lost our steel because of this," said one voice.

"I lost three brothers trying to break down the fortress gates," another.

GabuKe waved these complaints away with a calm hand. "There is nothing to be gained by holding grudges over this. Not one of us has profited from this conflict."

"Perhaps not, but some have lost far more than others! As there are not enough Steelmen for all the tribes, I propose that this can be our recompense."

This suggestion gained a great deal of support, and no lack of scorn.

"And what of the interpreter?" shouted someone else. "If he lives, who will have his voice? He can speak everything the others know, and this is better than ten silent hands."

"Let only those who fought with honour have the steel!" bellowed Tribe-father, standing by the fire. "Should we let these 'friends' have swords, who bought them from the tyrant?"

"Better than to give them to the KasseKo!"

Tribe-father lunged towards the speaker, one finger jabbing the air. "We lost more warriors than you in that great battle! We didn't have the tyrant's shields to keep us safe!"

Any support this gained from the surrounding KasseKo was drowned out by BaraKa, shouting from the front. "If you envy anyone here, remember the SalaKo, whose warriors all fell at the foot of the fortress, and the BataKo, too, who were lost to the ash. None remain to weep for them."

The vast crowd, suddenly, became silent.

GabuKe took up his speech again: "It is only natural to want new battles. Battles to replace wealth or honour that we have lost. But the whole island waged this war. Anyone who launches such an attack must be aware that other tribes doubtless hold the same grudges against them. This war has had a heavy cost: more fighting will not win it back."

SutaKe stood. Though his face was not so well recognised as GabuKe's—was not even visible—this part was his to say. "Those of you who joined the HoluKo before the battle, and those who came when it was done. GabuKe is right: much blood has been spilled, and further violence can never restore it to the tribes. But it is not enough that this war simply end. If the Steelmen come here again, who can say that this will not be repeated? We must remain together, remain strong. Then, if other merchants come, they must make honest trades or face the wrath of all the tribes."

This was met with a unanimous cheer. Even the tribesmen of the KasseKo joined in. And yet two of that great number were still not moved. When the noise died down, Tribe-mother and Tribe-father stood. "This," said Tribe-mother, "is not our way. We do not choose to concern ourselves with the squabbles and dealings of the coastal tribes or any who live beyond the mountain's foot. However, by this token you may be sure that the KasseKo will make no bargains with foreign merchants. It is not in our nature to be an enemy to any one tribe, but neither can we be a friend to all."

This darkened the mood of the meeting, and more angry chatter rose up, particularly from the DanaKo. The KasseKo were not, it was true, a threat to any one tribe in particular, but their past service to the warlock and their unprovoked attacks made them an unwelcome neighbour to every tribe.

"If the rest of the island chooses to band together," BaraKa spoke loudly enough for the whole crowd to hear, "you would be wise to show good will by doing the same. You have no allies otherwise, and the united coast would be a formidable enemy to you indeed." This little speech gained great support from the surrounding tribes.

Beneath his two-skull mask, the corners of Tribe-father's mouth fell. Still, he displayed none of the forceful rage that he had done before. "We do not concern ourselves with these trivial things. We guard the mountain with a greater cause in mind."

The hands of the KasseKo strayed towards their spears. The chieftains of the other tribes began to seek out their warriors amongst the crowd.

"Wait!" SutaKe stood once more. Almost before he was even on his feet, he had realised what he had to say. "Tribe-mother. Tribe-father. The things our people want are not at odds. Come with me to the warlock's cave, and I will show you how we share your cause. Bring hammers and wedges, levers and mauls: we will have need of them when we arrive."

Without delay, SutaKe, Tribe-father, and Tribe-mother—and a large group of followers—left the feast and began the journey to the cave, even in the fading light of day. GabuKe had the ember log still, and he filled and took this so that they could have light quickly when they arrived. It was dark before they reached the mountain path, though even now SutaKe could remember the small landmarks that he had seen before. He was glad of this, for not even Tribe-mother or Tribe-father could pick their way along the winding trail by moonlight alone.

SutaKe did not pause to look around the cave this time, but stepped right over RanaZo's clutter to the back, where solid rock gave way to piled stones. "Here." He placed a hand in the gap between loose rock and cave wall. "Lever these out."

This elicited cries and prayers from the KasseKo.

"This cave holds powerful magic," explained Tribe-mother. "No member of our tribe would dare disturb it."

"Very well." SutaKe took a wooden pole from one of the DanaKo. "BaraKa?"

The warrior said nothing, but shuffled back into the crowd, a look of shame upon his face.

"KanaKa." SutaKe stepped towards him. "A warrior who has fought the KasseKo need fear nothing else." He smiled, forgetting once again that he was wearing the obsidian mask.

"What the KasseKo themselves fear," said KanaKa deliberately, "would be better left alone."

For a moment, SutaKe faltered, wondering if this really was the right thing to do.

"The KasseKo mean well with their reverence," the spirit whispered in his ear, "but they have forgotten why it is they guard this place. Only let them remember, only show them, and I give my word they will be grateful."

Trusting the spirit, and thinking of HanaRa, SutaKe pushed the pole in beside the rock and proceeded to work it from its place. The stones had been stacked with great skill, and they interlocked tightly with one another. It was difficult work. But once the first stone tumbled—forcing SutaKe to jump aside to save his feet—other warriors came forward to take their share of the work. In the weedy light of GabuKe's fire, supplemented by rushlights he had had the sense to bring, they cleared a space just big enough for one man to pass through, if he turned his shoulders sideways.

SutaKe squeezed through this gap. "A light." He stretched his hand back through. "Give me a light."

GabuKe passed over a small bundle of new rushlights, followed by one already lit. Careful not to drag the fuel away from the flame, SutaKe carried the burning light smoothly, stepping out of the gaze of the fire in the cave, and into the darkness beyond.

The way his footsteps sounded on the smooth stone floor told SutaKe that this was a large space, and fairly regular in shape. He hugged the wall, unwilling to step out into the centre when the burning reed offered only that shallow pool of light. The darkness was like a sea, and he had no idea what lurked within its greatest depths. One hand on the wall for guidance, he felt his fingers drop into the corner of an alcove. Shining his faint light into it, he saw three skulls, their teeth filed like those of RanaZo.

"Follow their gaze." The spirit's voice did not whisper in his ear. It spoke from somewhere inside the room.

Moving away from the skulls and towards the voice, SutaKe pushed forward into the darkness. The air was stuffy, and his rushlight began to gutter. Just as a precaution, he lit a second, holding it in that same hand. Wraiths of smoke wound sluggishly through the lifeless air. SutaKe moved with tedious grace, unable to see what lay beneath his feet. There was something soft and powdery on the floor here—wood ash, perhaps—and he was wary of stumbling into a brazier or fire pit. His caution was well-warranted. Soon, a carved pedestal lurched from the darkness. There was a hollow in it with holders for two rushlights. Taking two fresh ones, he placed these in the spaces provided and lit them from the others. The first light, he threw away: it had burned too short to use.

Looking about, wondering if he had strayed from the path of the skulls' gaze, he saw the edge of a stone altar like the one he had found in the ruined temple. Stepping closer, he saw that not only was it intact, there was tinder, wood and kindling set out inside, ready to burn. Putting the flame of his rushlight to it, the ancient pyre flared up quickly. He turned back towards the pedestal, and there he saw the spirit.

Carved from stone, it sat and stared. It took SutaKe a

moment to realise that its blazing eyes were the rushlights he had left, standing in the hollow of its head. The altar fire showed that the carving of the pedestal provided arms, torso, folded legs. This was the spirit's idol, and the thing the KasseKo had guarded all these years.

"Is that you?" SutaKe stepped forwards. He recognised the spirit from the In-between, but still could not be sure that this truly was its body: the place it had been housed.

"It is me, SutaKe, and your work is almost done."

"Do you speak to us?" KanaKa's voice came in through the entrance and echoed off the walls. "I could not make out what you said."

"Call them in," the spirit said to SutaKe. "Tell them how I stirred the mountain."

SutaKe did as he was asked. "Come inside and bring the KasseKo," he called out to KanaKa. "They will want to see this most of all." KanaKa and GabuKe pushed through the gap—GabuKe with some difficulty—but though Tribe-mother and Tribe-father followed, the rest of the KasseKo remained outside, their whispered prayers alone drifting through into the chamber.

KanaKa coughed. If there had ever been a chimney when this place was new, it was blocked now, and the smoke from the fire was already filling the still air.

SutaKe spoke to Tribe-mother. "You said that you guarded the mountain for a great cause. I think that this is it."

Tribe-mother studied the intricate carving of the idol, the perfect proportions of its arms and legs. "There are legends concerning such a thing," was all she said.

"This represents the spirit that came to our aid in that hopeless battle. These are the hands that opened the mountain and sent out the ash. This spirit helped the coastal tribes. It shared our cause. Would it not be only right, then, for you to support us, and us you?"

Tribe-father spoke. "Had this been shown to us any

other way, I would have thought it to be some new trick. But I have seen the flame on the mountain, and I know no other way you could have found this place that even we had lost. If it is the spirit's will, we shall join the coastal tribes, and grow our people into an empire beyond the bounds of tradition, and our old ways."

"This is good," the spirit whispered, "but still my sacred places lie in ruins."

SutaKe was about to say something, but Tribe-mother spoke before he had a chance. She wrinkled her nose. "There is much to be done here. This place lies in ruins and in darkness. If the spirit has returned, we must bring light into the temple, must unblock what windows it may have. Always must this fire burn, and always must rushlights stand ready to fuel these eyes."

And for almost the first time since he put on that obsidian mask, SutaKe was truly happy. The spirit had served him well in times of war, but it was only now, in peace, that the fate he coveted could ever be attained.

26
THE GREAT WORK

In the weeks that followed, a great deal of work was done. Though the tribes separated once more—each returning to their own fires and their own fields—all did their part to restore the spirit's works to their former glory. The pillars in the temple of the DanaKo valley stood tall once more, and though the roof had crumbled and rotted long ago, a new one took its place, formed of good, straight tree trunks and lashed together with the strongest cord.

Other temples, too, were found out in the brush. Ruins known only as hunters' landmarks were cleared of squeezing vine and pushing fern and furnished with new altars, new walls. SanaRo and Tribe-father worked side by side to craft new talismans of the mountain's black glass, commemorating the spirit's victory over the Steelmen. These tokens were taken by runners from all over the island and placed with ceremony in each temple and shrine.

The spirit's chamber, too, was swept, and its relics mended. Workmen of the KasseKo, well familiar with the mountain's sides, found the place above the fire where the smoke was to escape, and with long staves they cleared its path. Others walked about the chamber's walls, knocking at windows that had been filled in by ancient ash so that those on the outside could dig them clear. Even with these sun-passages open once again, the temple inside was not bright. But craftsmen at the marsh worked all day long to dip new rushlights, and others took stone axes to the forest, bringing wood back for the sacred fire, so that even at night the spirit's chamber was never dim.

This was the work of legend, yet with all the tribes united it was not hard. The KasseKo took freely from the HoluKo quarry, bringing the Stonemen all that they could use. With all welcome at the mountain's foot, journeys across the island took only half as long and so travel was not now the chore it had once been. The DanaKo, also, did their part. Their bountiful fields fed those who had left their crops to work on the mountain, restoring the chamber to the grandeur of old.

In this way, all the tribes supported one other as a single nation, guided by SutaKe. SutaKe in turn was guided by the spirit who had led him through the war. And SutaKe followed its guidance eagerly, because he knew that it would serve him well. Also, beyond this, SutaKe had come to pity the spirit. Though nobler than himself, possessing power no mortal man could match, it was as loyal as any of his warriors and put no price upon its aid. It had helped the HoluKo out of empathy alone, and the depth of its emotion had come to move SutaKe. It spoke often of how it had shaped the island—tended to all its creatures, seen that it was sustained—only to be overthrown by new gods and a new way, and altogether forgotten in the process. It was only fair, SutaKe thought, that it be rewarded. It was only fair that it be restored. But not everyone shared this view.

"SutaKe." HanaRa paused in her weaving—work that would furnish the spirit's chamber with hanging ornaments—to speak to the leader of the tribes.

"Yes?" With more followers now than any chief before, SutaKe should have had no time to talk, but still he could not ignore HanaRa. He had won the war for all the tribes, but his work in this time of peace was for her alone. Her, and the spirit who had served him so selflessly, and so had to be repaid.

Though it was she who had spoken first, she hesitated now before she could continue. "This new way worries me," she said, bluntly.

SutaKe also hesitated, but only to laugh. "Why should it worry you?" He wondered for a moment if she might only be thinking of some new way of weaving, but her face suggested otherwise. "Is something wrong?" he asked, growing serious again.

"No..." she looked down. "At least, not now. Only...we fought so hard to avoid the Steelman's rule. Had Oltak won, all the tribes would have had to serve his will. Rather than tending to our own tuber fields, we would have had to rely on the trader's goods for food, in exchange for work that served him and him alone."

SutaKe said nothing. What HanaRa said was true, but he was not sure why it mattered now.

"We fought hard to avoid that," she said, "but what we do now is the same. GabuKe feeds almost all the island under your instruction. The rest restore the ruins that you order, and build up shrines where you say."

Suddenly, SutaKe saw. "This is not something to worry about," he explained, kindly. "This will last for only as long as it takes to rebuild the estate of the spirit that offered help so freely in our last battle. After that, the tribes will join only in times of war. And that, I hope, will never be necessary."

"That is another thing that worries me. This spirit. The spirit that you spoke to once and must repay." HanaRa stepped close, trying to look back through the eyes of the mask. "People see and hear strange things when there is great work to be done, and grave penalties for failure. I worry for the tribes. But also, more so, I worry for you."

SutaKe placed a hand on her shoulder. "This is the most frivolous worry of all." But he could say no more to wave away her fears. He knew he could not tell how the spirit had helped before that last battle, how it had guided every path he took as chief. His rule as SutaKe was already a charade: to tell of all the spirit's aid would prove it altogether false. "Tribe-mother and Tribe-father and GabuKe all believe that it was the spirit who brought ash down from the mountain. All the chieftains do. And besides: you said you would support me, too."

"I made that promise before I knew of this. But I will keep it still. Only remember what you set out to do."

"I will." Already, SutaKe was thinking of what success the spirit's plan might bring. "I will."

27
THE MASK RESTORED

Before long, the work for the spirit was almost complete. Lavish temples dotted the island, with shrines at holy loci drawn between. The spirit's chamber in the mountain had been furnished with the finest ornaments of obsidian, chipped and ground into shapes no other stone could hold. SanaRo's skill with the tools of his trade had grown considerably in the service of the spirit, and those items he had produced towards the end were far superior to his worthiest efforts at the beginning. The evidence was all around. Only a few shrines, in the most remote places, remained unfurnished.

Indeed, there was no part of the island that remained untouched by the spirit's guiding hand. A temple stood on every hill, a shrine in every valley, all in praise of the one who had secured the freedom of this place. As SutaKe walked the path to the spirit's chamber once again, he paused to look back and reflect on the obelisks of pumice that had been raised in a line up to the chamber entrance. This place, that had once been the desolate, untamed wasteland of the KasseKo was once again the hallowed heart of the island.

In the chamber, the spirit's idol sat, rushlight eyes glowing even in the flickering light of the altar fire. "Welcome, SutaKe. Good health to the tribes."

"And to you." SutaKe's reply was echoed a moment later by GabuKe, Tribe-mother and Tribe-father, who seldom left the chamber now.

"I see the work that has been done, and I am pleased. I do not know if I can ever recover all the strength that I once lost—so very long ago—but this at least will ease my pain. I was glad when you came to the warlock's cave because I knew you would be an ally. Now, in this chamber, I am overjoyed because I know you are not only this: you are a friend. It brings me solace to be unforgotten. It brings me joy that I am not alone. Thank you, SutaKe."

"Your thanks honour me, but also I am ashamed." SutaKe stepped in past the sacred fire. "You should know that I was not entirely selfless in my work. There is one gift I had yet hoped to gain from you."

"Yes." The spirit's eyes popped and crackled. "But send the others from the room. There is much that we alone must discuss."

SutaKe turned to speak, but Tribe-mother was already guiding the others to the door. Following without instruction, the few men still working in the chamber chose this time, respectfully, to take their leave.

"What is it?"

"I have thought deeply about this peacetime problem. Always, since that final battle at the Steelman's fortress—and even before—it has remained in the back of my mind. More recently, I have given it my full attention. But always when I think on it, I must consider that great barrier that you already see: the chieftain of your tribe cannot stoop to consort with a commoner. Tradition forbids it, and honour too. And these ancient rules are just, because they ensure that the chief must forge a bond with another tribe, and only choose a wife whose station befits his own. These are the ways of the HoluKo, these have been the ways of eons past, and not even SutaKe can change them now."

SutaKe's heart dropped to the floor. He had hoped, at first, that he would find some hidden solution to this problem, that there would be some way around it. After that, when he had failed, he hoped that the spirit's eyes could see what his had not, that its mind could vault the wall that his could not. But now the spirit too had failed. More than ever, he empathised with its own great solitude. "Is there no way this can be done? Is there no sacrifice that I can make?"

"There is no way that SutaKe can do this thing." The spirit's voice was firm and uncrackling. "He must always be the immortal leader of the HoluKo. He must lead his warriors against any tribe that would threaten them. He must speak with any neighbour, no matter how terrible, who can stand beside them when more strength is needed. He must defend their land against any enemy from any shore."

"I see." SutaKe bowed his head, the great stone mask feeling heavier than ever it had done before.

"He must do these things," continued the spirit, forcefully. "And he is not you."

SutaKe looked up.

"You were wounded on the mountain. You know you can be slain! Is this not true?"

"It is."

"You did not stand against the DanaKo when they threatened your tribe. I had to guide you! Is this not true?"

"It is."

"You did not go to the KasseKo when they could offer aid. I had to lead you! Is this not also true?"

"It is." Inside the mask, SutaKe felt a tear spread across his cheek. The spirit spoke only what he had always known.

He was no sort of chieftain for the HoluKo.

"All these things I did for you, that SutaKe alone could do. You did not do them. I did. I ask you then: who is SutaKe?"

He paused. The eyes of the spirit in the idol glowed, and the fire flickered over grooves in its carved head. Grooves, he could see now, that matched the straps of his own mask. "You are," he whispered.

"Then give to me my face of glass."

With great care, he unfastened the straps. Then, reverently, he secured them over the stone head of the idol. Stepping back, he saw the smoke unfurl, the gazing light of the eyes now focused, directed by the obsidian mask. Once he had also given over the woven collar, he turned to leave, without even anything to hide his sorrow.

"Do not grieve over this." SutaKe's voice was clearer, sharper, more real now that he had his sacred mask once more. "You are no chieftain, it is true, but know that you have done well to lead the tribe. There is no shame in your acts, which were truly great for one of your low station: for you are only a commoner." He spoke kindly. "Think of what that means, and I doubt that you can grieve."

Realisation dawned suddenly. SutaKe could not consort with commoners, but he was no longer SutaKe. The impossible solution had come at last. "Then...who am I now?"

"That is hard to say. ParuMe was buried the day after the DanaKo came. You cannot have that name. Neither can you take mine, for I have never had one but that I bear now. You can have no name." SutaKe paused, then laughed, suddenly. "You can have NonaMe!"

It was a joke at his expense—the name of a slave—but NonaMe could hardly complain. To be a slave in name alone was still to be free, and for this great gift, he could still count himself lucky. "Thank you, SutaKe," he said. "You have done everything that I could not."

"And your work is finished. The KasseKo can speak for me now: they have waited long enough."

As NonaMe left the chamber, only KanaKa seemed to recognise him. But the warrior said nothing.

"The chieftain of the tribes is waiting inside," NonaMe said to the group by the entrance. "Your presence is requested."

Tribe-father nodded, but still nothing was said. The small group made their way solemnly back inside, followed by the little throng of workmen with small jobs still to be completed. NonaMe instead went down the mountain, following the zigzag line between the obelisks, still hardly able to believe what had happened. The tribe had been saved, the Steelmen vanquished, and now, the most joyous thing of all to him, he was free.

28
THE TRIBES UNITED

HanaRa was no longer weaving cords. Those decorations had been finished long ago, and now more people were needed in the tuber fields of the HoluKo. The spirit had required so many workers for the shrines and temples that the tribes' crops had withered and food would soon be in short supply. But all the weavers—and many of the unskilled workers of pumice and wood—had stepped in to help, and now NonaMe would be glad to do the same. As HanaRa stood and turned to stare at him, he suddenly realised he wasn't sure what to say.

She dropped her farming stave. "SutaKe?"

"No." he said, happily. "Of course not."

Heedless of tradition, she threw her arms around him. "I don't understand."

NonaMe whispered, lest the moon should hear. "I never really was the chief. It...I couldn't have told you before. Everything I did to save our people, everything I said to the other tribes...it was the spirit, really. I only did what it said to do, and every time it was the right thing. The spirit has the mask now. It is SutaKe. This is how things were always meant to be."

"I did think it strange that a fool like you could lead so well." She stepped out of the embrace and sniffed, tears of joy rolling down her cheeks.

NonaMe laughed. He knew only HanaRa would say that to his face, and only HanaRa would not mean what she said.

"So there really is a spirit, then?" she asked. "I was worried that was only in your mind. But I suppose stranger things have happened, in ancient days when the island was new. I know little about spirits, but I think I know enough about you."

For a week or two, NonaMe and HanaRa worked happily together in the fields. There was always a great deal to be done, and their tasks were hard, but in each other's company these hardships were easy to bear. Also, they knew that very soon the great work would be complete, and things would be just as they had been before, only safer, more peaceful, more secure. But after that brief, happy time, KanaKa came down from the mountain. He came bearing news.

"Tribe-mother and Tribe-father have spoken with the idol of SutaKe." He gave this speech by the village fire, though many of the HoluKo were still elsewhere. "They have been told that the temples are good, and the shrines are good, and the chamber is good. The leader of the tribes is pleased with these things."

There were agreeable mutterings from all around the fire. NonaMe and HanaRa smiled at one another, knowing that the great work had now come to an end. But KanaKa continued.

"But these things, SutaKe says, are not enough."

This time, the mutterings were not so approving.

"The people of the island have become powerful through unity, and SutaKe is powerful as well. A chieftain of such dignity, the KasseKo report, cannot be content with such a small domain. That is why it has been ordered that we build a fleet of boats, strong with outriggers, capable of carrying all the warriors of this place. With this fleet we will bring war to other islands, and to the vast land of the Steelmen, wherever it may be. With this fleet we will expand our empire, and rid ourselves of any future threat."

His message given, KanaKa took his place on one of the seating logs by the fire. But the outcry from the crowd was so loud that he was forced to stand once more. He raised both hands to placate them. "Friends, this is not the way I would have chosen. But the chieftain of the tribes has spoken and Tribe-mother, Tribe-father, GabuKe: all are in agreement. I do not like this myself, but it must be known that this early sacrifice will serve us well in years to come. I will not oppose it."

The crowd became positively feverish. HanaRa turned to NonaMe. "You must do something. This is like before, when the Steelman first came to make his offer. And it is like what would have been, had he not been toppled in that last battle. Go to the mountain! The spirit will listen to no one else."

"I..." NonaMe thought hard. "Would that really be for the best?"

"What are you saying?"

"This is the mind that led us through the war. When this began, we had nothing: only the warriors of our own tribe against all the island, and the Steelmen as well. With its guidance, we gained an ally in the DanaKo, and we crushed the foreign army of the Steelmen. With its guidance, we won an ally in the KasseKo. And with its power, we destroyed the army of the puppet-chiefs and scattered their supporters. I am nobody now, HanaRa. If the spirit wishes that these things be done, who am I to tell it otherwise? It has brought us such power, after all."

"What good is power if it only serves a tyrant?"

"Is it not good that it has brought us back together?" He leaned in close and smiled, but HanaRa pushed him roughly away.

"No!" she said, loud enough for the whole tribe to hear. "No, because now I know what I only suspected before. You are not the person I once knew. At first I was happy. At first I could pretend this was not so. But you have changed. Our tribe has emerged victorious from the war, but in this victory you have lost yourself."

"I have lost nothing but a name." NonaMe spread his arms imploringly.

"No." HanaRa shook her head. "It is more than that. Before, you may not have been all-knowing, you may not have been strong, but you would have done what needed to be done. The person who saved our tribe from one tyrant could not have sold it to another." She turned her back.

NonaMe looked around for support, as he had done when he wore the mask, but there was none. The other tribesmen looked at the ground, and some looked at the sky, wary that the moon might have heard, but none spoke in his favour. Indeed, none spoke at all. And NonaMe realised that he could not expect them to, because HanaRa was right. The strength she had brought out in him, he had long since given away to the idol in the mountain. With the KasseKo as its voice, the spirit's greed had grown as great as that of the Steelman, and he had handed it the island. Turning from the scene of his shame, he fled into the forest. Perhaps because he had walked it now so many times, he found himself upon the path to the mountain. Walking it once again, he saw the true barrier that he had faced: whether he or the spirit wore the mask of SutaKe, he and HanaRa could never be together. He had been a fool to think they could. There was only one thing left to do. Continuing along that familiar path, NonaMe made his slow way towards the mountain, and the flame-lit idol that waited inside.

29
THE NAME OF THE GODS

W hen NonaMe returned to the mountain, the work in the chamber had long been completed. The inside seemed bright now, illuminated by so many rushlights. The marsh, seen from the entrance, now looked bare, stripped of the reeds that would provide the spirit's light. But brightest of all were the eyes inside the mask. NonaMe approached, pausing only to steal a glance at Tribe-father—sitting below a shelf of skulls—now the only person to attend the spirit.

"SutaKe." He stepped before the idol and kneeled. "I have come to speak with you."

"That is not your place anymore." The masked spirit was blunt, but not unkind. "Are you not happy with the things that have been done? Do you think my gift to you was not enough?"

"I am not happy," answered NonaMe, "and your gifts have cost me dearly. But that is not why I have come."

"Then tell me, why have you come?"

NonaMe looked over at Tribe-father once more, but

though the idol's guardian stared back, he did not move. "I want to know if others hear your voice as I do. I want to know if what the tribe-leaders have ordered is truly what you wish."

SutaKe laughed. "You are not entirely foolish, NonaMe. You are right to question this, for though my power has grown, the others do not yet hear me speak. Fate brought you to me, and fate, so far, brings my voice to no ears but your own. But I have influence enough to make my wishes known. That which has been ordered, I have not ordered. However, that which will be done is what I wish to be done. This is my way, and this is my voice. The ambitions of the chieftains are my own."

Tribe-father stood. His footsteps echoed as he walked towards the chamber entrance, but he did not leave. Instead, he simply stood there in the centre of the door.

NonaMe turned back to the idol. "Then you do want another war? This really was your wish?"

"Yes."

"Then..."

SutaKe interrupted. "I do not need you to speak of your will. Your mind has told it to me like a tale. I know that you have come to claim my mask, and I tell you that I will not give it!"

NonaMe spoke in a low voice, hoping not to let Tribe-father hear. "You told me you were SutaKe. You convinced me you could lead the tribes. Now I know this is not so. SutaKe must always serve his people, but you serve only your own ambitions."

"And do I not deserve to do this? I made you strong where you were weak. Selflessly, I performed all the tasks that you could not. I have earned this power from you, and I have earned the right to use it as I wish!"

NonaMe could see that there was no convincing the spirit. Not in this way, at least. But through his trials, words had become familiar to him like a well-worn tool, and he knew now something of the Storyteller's art. "You told me time and time again of how new gods usurped your throne. You told me that you offered aid because in our plight, you saw your own. Why do you now wrong us in that same way?"

The voice behind the mask became a hiss. "Because it is right for me to do so! I told you time and time again of how new gods usurped my throne, but did I ever tell you their name?" The eyes flared brightly for a moment. "That name was Man."

Suddenly, NonaMe could see how the last trick had been played, and its method was familiar to him. "This is like SutaKe in the legends."

The rigid mask flickered with mirth. "And well familiar it should be! Did I not tell you at our last meeting? Did you not agree?" The voice chuckled. "I am SutaKe."

NonaMe could find no words to match this.

"I hold the power of Sun and Mountain! Moon ensures that I shall always live! I shaped this island, and for as long as I could sustain my presence in this world, I led my people. By what right could you claim my face? By what right could you use my name? You are no one, NonaMe." The voice became a whisper. "You are nothing."

An arm whipped around NonaMe's neck. Reacting instinctively, he tried to tug it away. Tribe-father's stone knife, instead of slicing into his throat, merely cut a notch in his shoulder. But still the warrior had a tight hold of NonaMe, and the knife remained dangerously close. Unable to duck forward out of his grip, NonaMe pushed back, standing with sudden force. Moving together, the two of them fell, but it was Tribe-father's back that found the searing stone of the altar fire, and so he pushed away. NonaMe fell sprawling to the floor. Recovering quickly, Tribe-father made a lunge with the knife, but from the floor NonaMe kicked as high as he could, leaving Tribe-father doubled over in pain.

NonaMe hurried to the back of the chamber, where darkness still reigned. When he recovered, Tribe-father remained staring out from the bath of light, trying to see past the rushlights' glow, trying to squeeze the fire glare from his eyes. In the darkness, NonaMe remained perfectly still, wondering what to do. He wished he'd thought to bring a weapon, but if the KasseKo hadn't stopped him at the foot of the mountain, Tribe-father would have stopped him in the chamber. Slowly, knife ready, Tribe-father began to venture farther back into the room.

NonaMe knew there would be no fighting him up close. Beyond the advantage of the knife, Tribe-father was a fearsome warrior, and NonaMe knew he had been exceptionally lucky to have survived this encounter for so long. Within his two-skull mask, Tribe-father's eyes darted methodically left and right in turn. Every one of his steps upon the stone was silent and perfectly steady. With practised ease, he flipped the blade within his hand, favouring whichever grip seemed to suit him best at any given moment. NonaMe remained still, pressed against the chamber wall now, his hand reaching into one of the alcoves.

In one smooth arc, NonaMe whipped the skull from its sacred place, sending it crashing into the bone surface of Tribe-father's mask. Tribe-father stumbled, clutching his eye where the mask had splintered but, more remarkably, SutaKe cried out. NonaMe hurled another skull as Tribe-father recovered. This one was well wide of the mark, but as it broke apart against the floor, SutaKe screamed.

As Tribe-father tried to brush the fragments from his eye, NonaMe found another trick weaving together, fibre by fibre. SutaKe's power had grown along with his followers. It had grown as the shrines and temples were restored. This knowledge gave NonaMe new strength. Making a dash before Tribe-father could recover, he reached the entrance to the chamber.

"Coward!" Tribe-father bellowed, tearing the ruined mask from his head. Spittle flecked his sparse beard. "Turn and fight me!"

But NonaMe had reached the thing that he had run for. By the doorway was a great stack of firewood, taken from the forest, and in this stack he found a long branch, sturdy and unrotten. Meeting Tribe-father's mad charge, he jabbed, rather than swung. Caught off-guard, Tribe-father had to flinch away to one side, and in this opening, NonaMe dealt his true strike. With both hands, he brought the branch around to meet the side of Tribe-father's head. Without waiting to see if his enemy was stunned, he took the branch to every skull in every alcove, every ornament on every cord. SutaKe's screams increased in volume, punctuated by hollow pleas.

"I will make a bargain with you. The power of Mountain can be yours, if only you will stop."

NonaMe plucked SutaKe's mended sword from the idol's hand and tossed it into the altar fire. Obsidian blades cracked in the sudden heat.

"Then Sun. Think of the wealth that could be yours! Only stop this."

NonaMe said nothing. He tore the woven collar from the idol's neck. This too, he tossed into the flames.

"I will give you everything," SutaKe whispered. "Mountain. Sun. What I have of Moon. Only..."

NonaMe set the branch into the idol as a lever, lifting with all his strength until it toppled and smashed. But still the voice spoke. SutaKe could not make out words, but it buzzed. It buzzed like the wings of a thousand insects. The mask stared up at him from its place on the floor, a fragment of rushlight still glowing in an eye. NonaMe took up a piece of the idol itself and hefted it, ready to cast down upon the face.

"Stop!" Tribe-father struggled to stand, but could no longer balance. His left eye was swollen shut. "Stop," he said, one feeble arm outstretched. "Please...it holds such power."

Even beyond its magic, the mask was a marvel. Seeing the way its polished darkness caught and threw the firelight, NonaMe considered that no other could ever be made. He considered also how long he had worn it over his own face. The mask was priceless beyond measure. Bearing this in mind, he etched every inch of it into his memory as it smashed. He saw the cheekbones buckle and spin. He saw the grains of glass that leapt in the light of the flames, and those that clung to the rock as it bounced and rolled out into the darkness. "What good is power," he asked Tribe-father, "if it only serves a tyrant?"

As he walked briskly out into the open air, NonaMe paused to clutch at his wound. The cut inflicted by Tribe-father's knife did not seem serious, but it had scored over the place where the arrow had struck him, still not quite healed. Covering it with a hand, NonaMe felt something prickle beneath his skin. Ignoring the stab of pain as he did so, he drew it out. It was a shard of bone. After a brief, sickening moment while he thought it was his own, he remembered the arrowhead: long like a dagger, carved from bone. This fragment, this little fragment of that great thing, had remained buried all that time. Carelessly, he tossed it down the side of the mountain, towards the very place it had been loosed from the bowstring. Nevermore would he return to that chamber in the mountain, and nevermore would the spirit speak into his ear.

With this small gesture, the great work was done.

30
EYES LIKE FLAME

*I*n ancient days when the island was new, a great crocodile came
to rest upon the southern shore. It was a vast creature, long as
a boat and with skin as hard as stone. The scent of the
crocodile panicked all the creatures of the forest. Its footsteps drove all
the birds up to the peak of high mountain. Its breath withered the
leaves of the people's crops, and turned the tubers black. The crocodile
had teeth like spearheads and claws like stakes, and its eyes glistened
like pearls.

Before long, a hunter came to drive away the crocodile. But his
arrows rattled off its scales, and he dared not draw close enough to use
his club, so terrible were that beast's jaws. Seeing the creature then, he
knew that no number of warriors could move it from its place. But as
he wandered home, dismayed, he heard a voice from up a tree.

"Your plight moves me, hunter," hissed the voice. The hunter saw
it belonged to a little green snake, high in the branches, eyes like tiny
flames. "Already I am driven from the ground, for fear of that great
beast that has come upon the island. Carry me upon your shoulders,
and I shall see you do not share my fate."

The hunter, knowing that he had no other chance, did as the

serpent asked.

The little creature curled its tail around his neck and whispered in his ear: "The crocodile may be strong, but I am cunning. Have your wife weave a sturdy cord, plaited tight and of great thickness. This is how it must be done."

So the hunter did as the serpent asked, and his wife's cord was sturdy indeed, for she knew the strength of the crocodile and was skilled at weaving. As she worked, the serpent watched with eyes like flame, waiting on the hunter's shoulders because it feared the ground.

When the cord was woven, the serpent spoke again: "Now seek out a place of pumice not far from the shore, and set your cord out as a snare."

So the hunter did as the serpent asked. It took many days to find the place—a great outcrop of rough stone, within sight of the water's edge—but it was exactly as the serpent said. With eyes like flame, it watched as he performed his work.

When the snare was set, the serpent spoke again: "Now hunt a boar, and set its carcass out before the snare."

So the hunter did as the serpent asked, and the serpent clung tightly around his neck, watching always with eyes like flame. Soon, the hunter found a boar. He loosed his arrows into its flesh, then followed as its life ran out. At last, the carcass was brought to the snare, and the hunter threw drops of blood out across the ground, so the crocodile would catch its scent and come looking.

The hunter watched as the beast came crawling across the ground, and the serpent watched too, with eyes like flame. Approaching from the shore, the crocodile set its teeth into the boar, and the snare tightened around its neck. It struggled to free itself, but as its claws scrabbled against the rough stone, they became blunt and powerless.

"Now!" hissed the serpent from the hunter's shoulders. "Strike now, and free us both from the sea-beast that has come!"

So the hunter did as the serpent asked. He stepped in behind the thrashing jaws, braved the blunted talons, and beat his club against the stony head. Once, twice, thrice, he drove down blows. At the third strike, his good club splintered, and the beast was dead.

But no sooner had the hunter killed the crocodile, the little snake's *body tightened around his neck, stopping the wind that fed his lungs. "Did you think I only feared the crocodile?" hissed the serpent. "It was you, with farming stave and trampling feet, who first drove me to the trees."*

The hunter saw then how he had been tricked, and how the snake had never been a friend. Carrying it around his neck, as he had done through all their trials, he ran out across the shore and pushed its head beneath the waves. Thus, in the water from which the crocodile had come, the eyes of flame were soon extinguished.

And this is why we should always be wary of those who offer aid, because even if their pains are like our own, their ambitions may be different indeed.

As NonaMe came to the end of his tale, there were approving chatterings from the small crowd in the temple on the hill. It was not one of the old legends. It told of no great battles and held no magic. But despite this, he thought the little gathering had recognised its significance, and he hoped that in years to come it would still be told, even when it could not be known what grain of truth had sparked it, nor what embellishments been added since. He had spent a week preparing it, fixing it into his memory, but still there would be much work to do. He looked to the Stoneman, SanaRo, sitting nearby with the tools of his trade. A broken figurine of glass lay to his left, a small cluster of arrowheads to his right: this temple was closer to the village than the quarry, and would supply him with materials for weeks to come. He finished pressing flakes from the edge of a blade, waiting for the conversation to die down.

At last, SanaRo paused in his work. "It is a good tale," he said, "albeit a short one. I wonder if you could not have made more of the crocodile—perhaps some nearby chieftains come to serve it, because it gives them scales to use as spearheads—but it is good so far as it goes."

This was all that NonaMe had hoped to hear. "Thank you, SanaRo. That means much, as you were a good

Storyteller for so long." He sat and stared up at the wooden roof of the temple on the hill, feeling the last warmth of the day wash away into the cool stones of the floor.

"You will have much work ahead of you," SanaRo warned. "It is usual that one Storyteller passes to the next his stock of tales, but many of mine can no longer be told. They concern that ancient hero, of whom we now refuse to speak."

"But surely there are others you could share..."

"None that other tribes do not already have." SanaRo spoke firmly. "The KasseKo are as terrible a foe as ever, and little keeps them tethered to the mountain. KanaKe will have greater need of allies, I think, than any chief before. It has always been the Storyteller who unites two tribes."

That was true, NonaMe thought, but he could not help but feel that the KasseKo were not the threat they once had been. Their ancient calling lost, many of the warriors had gone to other tribes, and though the KasseKo had long been feared for their savagery, he knew that even they would hesitate to attack their former tribesmen. Such a battle, he knew, none could truly win. In this respect, he thought, the HoluKo were safe: no small number of KasseKo had come to them, and even Tribe-father, despite his rage, would not be keen to turn against old friends.

Though the other tribes were no longer strong allies, neither were they foes. The DanaKo, at least, were still firm friends with the HoluKo, and GabuKe was going to great lengths to restore the unity of the tribes, lest the Steelmen should land again. Those who had come on the Red Turtle were no longer treated with the importance that they had been at the meeting by the mountain. The Stonemen of every tribe were becoming skilled with steel—preserving its shine and restoring its edge—but more than this, those blades no longer mattered. In bartering for things lost in the war and during the spirit's great work—tubers and fishing nets, rushlights and cord—steel arms and armour had been scattered all across the island, and now no tribe could hold that advantage over another.

In the last light of the day, as the group made their way back towards the village, NonaMe looked out from the temple towards the sea, and around at the surrounding hills. The sunlight sparkled on the water, and from the talismans in the three shrines he could see from this high place. He smiled to see them. These things were a beauty now, though it was only the wind that played through their beads and cords: there were no spirits left to claim their power now. Already, hands like SanaRo's had plucked some of the baubles from these sacred sites, and they feared no retribution. But while they held their roofs and treasures, the shrines were pleasing to the eye, and the temples were a good cool shelter from the flaring sun.

But still there was no better place to rest than a strong reed hut. NonaMe was happy to find that he could see his own from the side of that hill, though he would always feel a certain fondness for the little storeroom built onto its side. HanaRa slipped her arm into his, and they walked together back to the village that would always be their home. And as they walked, they spoke no words, because there was nothing left to be said, and here this story is done.

ABOUT THE AUTHOR

Damon L. Wakes was born in 1991 and began to write a few years later. In 2012, he graduated from the University of Reading with a degree in English Literature. He produces both short stories and novels, and particularly enjoys crafting new worlds. He has travelled from the blazing heat of Death Valley to the frozen peak of the Hockenhorn, but the only volcano he has seen for himself is in Iceland.

damonwakes.wordpress.com

Printed in Poland
by Amazon Fulfillment
Poland Sp. z o.o., Wrocław